Dear Readers,

Rake the leaves. Put up the storm windows. Get the sweaters out of mothballs. Start planning the Halloween costumes. But save lots of time for reading our four new Bouquet romances.

Pull the afghan up over your knees and settle down for a heart-stopping read with Marcia Evanick's **Somewhere in the Night**. Years ago, clairvoyant Bridget MacKenzie "saw" a harrowing crime in her dreams. Now, the nightmare is back, so she turns to Detective Chad Barnett to find a vicious killer . . . who is about to strike again. But solving the crime is only the beginning for Bridget and Chad. Next comes the fulfillment of an irresistible passion.

In Lynda Sue Cooper's **Unguarded Hearts,** a beautiful professional bodyguard is assigned to protect a threatened pro-basketball coach. Posing first as his "girlfriend," then as his "wife," Nina soon finds that keeping Mitch safe is only part of her job. Once his body is out of danger, it's time to guard his heart.

Everybody loves a cowboy, and Sarah Keller is no exception . . . even when her fantasy cowboy roars onto the ranch in a flashy sportscar. But city slicker Cole Jaegar quickly learns to savor life's simple pleasures in Connie Keenan's appealing Montana love story **And Then Came You**.

Who can resist a story about a wedding? Lynda Simmons's **Perfect Fit** will thrill readers with its charming heroine—wedding dress designer Rachel Banks—and its reluctant hero—international news cameraman Mark Robison. He's in town for his sister's wedding . . . or so he thinks until he meets Rachel . . . and begins to picture a wedding of his own.

Munch a bright red apple, carve a pumpkin, mull some cider, and leave the sugar and spice to us. We'll deliver it between the pages of these autumn Bouquets. Enjoy!

The Editors

A KISS GOOD NIGHT

"Thanks for dinner." Chad opened the door, but didn't step out onto the porch. He stood there and stared at her face for a long time. With a tender touch he traced a line down her cheek. "You have a streak of pink paint here."

"Iced Raspberry." She sighed as the warmth of his finger caressed her cheek and she felt light-headed. It was either a reaction from his touch or the paint fumes. She knew where she would bet her money.

Chad slowly smiled and that heated look returned to his eyes she had once classed as ordinary brown. She now knew better. They were deep chocolate with flecks of gold. "Thank you, Bridget." His voice sounded rough and uneven.

"For what?"

"For giving me an enjoyable evening. For talking about ordinary stuff and taking my mind off the case for a couple of hours." Chad brushed back a lock of hair that had escaped her ponytail. Her mouth went dry with anticipation. Chad was going to kiss her—she could see it in his eyes. . . .

SOMEWHERE IN THE NIGHT

MARCIA EVANICK

Zebra Books
Kensington Publishing Corp.

http://www.zebrabooks.com

ZEBRA BOOKS are published by

Kensington Publishing Corp.
850 Third Avenue
New York, NY 10022

First Printing: October, 1999
10 9 8 7 6 5 4 3 2 1

Printed in the United States of America

ONE

The dark alley glistened with freshly fallen rain. Oil-slickened puddles dotted the ground, along with garbage and soggy cardboard boxes. Metal dumpsters overflowed with trash, and the smell of rotting food permeated the chilly, damp air. A dog was barking in the distance. Nearby, a rodent scurried away.

Bridget Erin Mackenzie knew she was dreaming and forced herself to relax into the mist. It was the same dream she'd had for four nights straight. Each night it became clearer. The vision became more intense, more real. Tonight she could smell the decaying food and feel the damp chill against her heated skin. She prayed for the mist to release its secrets. She needed to know the location of the alley.

A lone man walked cautiously into the alley. Dark pants. Dark shoes. A dark rain poncho with something written on the back. Too dark to see. A dimly lit bulb dangled from some frayed wire at the other end of the alley. Gusts of wind brought by the recent shower made the bulb swing slowly back and forth. Shadows. Light. Shadows. Light.

Dented and rusted doors coated with graffiti lined both sides of the alley. Most of the doors had chains and heavy padlocks barring entry, or possibly someone's exit. Grime and graffiti covered cinder block and brick walls that rose two stories high. Darker squares attested to windows, but light shone from none. Danger filled every corner, and hatred reeked like a living beast.

The scene slowly unfolded before Bridget. She knew she couldn't escape it. Her only hope was to search the alley for clues to its location. Thousands of alleys just like this one littered the city. Philadelphia was known as the City of Brotherly Love. This was anything but brotherly and had nothing to do with love. Somewhere in the heart of the city a murder was about to take place, and she couldn't even figure out where it was going to happen. Little Italy? Chinatown? Some out-of-the-way alley in Society Hill?

Maybe she should stop trying to figure out where and concentrate on who. Last night when the dream had come, she had been drawn to the man's eyes when the gun blast shattered the dream. His brown eyes had held the knowledge he was going to die.

She didn't want to look into those eyes again. Instead, she concentrated on trying to read the back of the rain poncho.

The man slowly walked to the other end of the alley. Black shoes stepping over puddles. A head covered in dark hair turning right, left, and back to the right. He was cautious, as if he, too, sensed the danger.

The wind picked up and the lightbulb swung wildly. The man's rain slicker billowed and twisted in the wind, giving only glimpses of white letters. He reached the end of the alley and turned as if startled.

The rodents had stopped scurrying, but distant barking still echoed through the mist. Closer, tires raced across wet asphalt and somewhere a horn sounded—normal city sounds on a not-so-normal night. The swinging bulb lighted the man's features, then quickly cast them into shadows.

Bridget followed the man's movements instead of his eyes. She never wanted to see the look of impending death in a man's eyes again.

The man reached beneath the slicker, beneath the sports jacket below it, and into a holster. White pinstriped shirt. A tie with Road Runner on it. A gleam of metal. A gun appeared in his hand, but he wasn't quick enough. A gun blast shattered the night before his gun could fully clear the holster. The force of the blast jerked the man's arm and the gun slipped from his fingers. Wind plastered the raincoat against his chest. As the mist obscured the vision, there was one last glimpse of the poncho and the white letters neatly printed on the left breast pocket.

Directly above the man's heart.

A scream tore from Bridget's throat. "No!" Her arms flailed wildly as if trying to catch the bullet and change the dream's outcome. Sheets twisted around her arms and she knocked a pillow to the floor before she opened her eyes and stared up at her bedroom ceiling. Her harsh breathing and the thunder of her heart broke the silence of the night. A sense of doom and hopelessness settled on her trembling shoulders.

The curse had returned.

She knew what she had just experienced hadn't been a dream. It hadn't even been a nightmare. It was the truth. It was the future. The curse was back, and nothing she could do would stop it.

With a violent kick, she sent the comforter tumbling to the floor, pulled her knees up to her chest, and buried her face in her trembling hands. Warm tears soaked her fingers as the vision replayed itself again and again through her mind. She had silently prayed for an answer, and now she had one. The mist had given her one small fleeting glimpse of an answer. She didn't know who he was, but now she knew what he was. The man who was going to die was a police officer. The white letters on his poncho had read *Philadelphia Police Department.*

Grandmom Rosalie would be proud of her for the way she had searched the vision for clues, not fought it as she had when she was a little girl. Her grandmother had been the only member of the family who had understood the frightened little girl she had been. Grandmom had suffered the same fears. With fierce hugs, gentle hands, and a sweet voice that still betrayed her Irish roots, Grandmom Rosalie had explained about the gift that had been passed down for generations to the chosen few. Rosalie had called it by many names: *the sight, the foretelling, foresight, the second sight,* and even *prophecy.* The now seventy-two-year-old Rosalie had never called it by the name Bridget had given it: *the curse.*

Bridget couldn't ignore the visions any longer. They were coming too close together. Night after night, they had sucked her into the horror of watching an innocent man die. The intensity of the vision had mushroomed until she felt as if she had been standing in the alley with the officer. The vision was about to come true, and she was left to try the impossible. Grandmom Rosalie was going to fret up a storm. If she had told Bridget once, she had told her a million times the future was not theirs to change. Bridget knew she could not sit back and allow an officer of the law or any other human being to get gunned down in an alley. She had to try to change the future.

Hope did not fill her soul as she pushed back the rest of the sheet and climbed out of bed, but purpose did. She couldn't possibly track down one policeman in a city the size of Philadelphia. But she knew where to begin her search—with the one man who would believe her. A man she hadn't seen for five years, since the last time the visions disturbed her sleep and she had wanted to stop the horrors. A man who had saved her life, seen her at her worst and who had walked away without a backward glance. A man she had been halfway in love with before their world had come crashing down.

Detective Chad Barnett might want to put her and their past behind him, but he wouldn't turn her away. He would believe.

She knew many people did not believe in precognitive clairvoyance, but she had made a believer out of Chad. It had nearly cost her her life.

Bridget's fingers trembled as she pulled back her bedroom curtains. She stared out into the night and gently touched the only visible scar left from that night five years ago. With the tip of one finger, she slowly traced the thin pale line encircling her throat. Horrible, humiliating, and frightful memories threatened to overcome her, but she pushed them to the dark corners of her mind where they belonged and concentrated on the present. Grandmom Rosalie insisted she couldn't change the future. Bridget wasn't a hundred percent certain that was true, but she was positive she couldn't change the past. Why dwell on things that only hurt?

She shook off the memories and studied the darkness beyond her window. It was a clear, chilly late September night. No puddles or moisture darkened the streets or sidewalks. Hopefully the weather would hold throughout the night. No rain meant the vision wouldn't come true tonight. The officer wouldn't die tonight, but he would die soon—if she couldn't stop it.

The curtain fell back into place as she turned from the window and hurried toward the bathroom. It wasn't quite midnight yet. Surely it wouldn't be that hard to find Chad Barnett. Five years ago, the handsome young detective had never seemed to sleep. Surely he couldn't have changed that much.

Thirty minutes later, Bridget stared at the brass numbers on the door directly in front of her and then back down to the slip of paper clutched in her hand. Number three-o-five. It might be the wrong time, but she was in the right place—the first step toward changing the future. She stared at the plastic and brass button next to the door and prayed for the strength to see this through. Once she started the ball rolling, there would be no stopping it. Visions of reading the morning paper over her first cup of coffee and finding an article about the slain officer gave her the strength to push the doorbell.

The chimes echoed faintly throughout the apartment beyond the door, and once again she thought of the man who lived there. Five years hadn't seemed like a lot of time when she had driven over here, but now she realized how much he could have changed. Look how much she had changed.

The last time she had seen Chad Barnett, she had been a senior in college and unsure which path in life she would take. Five years later, she owned her own business and a small house in need of lots of love and attention, but which was in a nice neighborhood on a beautiful tree-lined street.

Faint rustling from the apartment reached her ears. For the first time, she wondered if Chad lived alone. With his boyish good looks, surely he had a girlfriend or even a significant other. Hell, for all she knew there could be a wife and a couple of babies behind the door. She was going to feel like a fool trying to explain to Chad's wife about this midnight visit and like a bigger fool if she woke any sleeping babies.

The sound of a chain being released from the back of the door caused her to square her shoulders. Even if she wanted to, it was too late to go hide from the visions and the future. The ball had already started to roll. It had started to roll the day she was born.

The man who opened the door was definitely Chad Barnett—an older, harder Chad Barnett. The gentle, boyish looks of a twenty-five year old had hardened on the man before her. The last five years hadn't been easy on him. The flare of recognition in his brown eyes made her feel somewhat better. At least he remembered her.

"Bridget?" Chad's sleep-roughened voice caused a jolt of awareness to slither down her backbone and pool in her abdomen. What was it about his voice that always had that effect on her?

She gave him a halfhearted smile. "You shouldn't open your door without asking who it is first, detective." For the short time she had known Chad, he had pounded, drilled, and then hammered more safety tips into her already paranoid brain. She sadly shook her head. "You didn't even leave the chain on."

Chad seemed to be studying every inch of her face. She knew what he would find. Exhaustion, paleness, fear, and probably signs of her earlier tears. Chad had always been exceedingly observant, and she hadn't bothered to hide the signs of her visions. He was going to find out about them soon enough.

"I'm a cop, Bridget. I can protect myself." Chad pulled his gaze away from her face and glanced up and down the deserted hallway. "The question is, why are you out alone at this time of the night?"

She had no doubt he could protect himself. Even dressed in nothing but a pair of tight-fitting jeans that were only halfway zipped and not even buttoned, Chad could protect himself. Fine dark hair sprinkled his well-defined chest and narrowed its way down to the gaping waistband of the worn jeans. She would bet every long-stemmed rose in her shop the only thing he had on under those jeans was warm skin.

She forced her gaze away from Chad's body and glanced over his shoulder to the empty apartment behind him. No wife in a clinging negligee to demand what lunatic was ringing their doorbell in the middle of the night, but the absence of a woman's presence didn't mean one wasn't warming his bed.

Her gaze met his as she gave him the simple truth. "They're back."

Chad didn't have to ask what. By the look on his face, he already knew. Impatient, he ran his fingers through his short brown hair, messing it even more. Chad looked like he would rather be anywhere else than here. She couldn't blame him. Her voice held an unspoken apology. "I had to come, Chad."

Too many emotions warred in his eyes for her to pick out just one. "Why?" His voice held confusion, fear, guilt, and regret in one massive ball.

She almost turned around and left. How could she do this to him again? How could she not? She didn't know what to say besides, "I'm sorry." Two simple words that sounded so inadequate.

"Why?"

He wasn't asking why she was sorry. He already knew, as she knew, why she was sorry for showing up on his doorstep. She was about to drag him into a living hell again. Maybe this time neither one of them would be lucky enough to escape with their lives. "You'll believe me, Chad. You of all people know I'm not crazy or making this up."

"Why now?" Chad's left hand was hooked casually on the pocket of his jeans, giving him a nonchalant appearance. His right hand gripped the door jamb with such force his knuckles had turned white. Chad had always been full of contradictions. "Why so long?"

"I don't know." Hard questions she had no easy answers to. "I thought the visions were gone for good." *I prayed the visions were gone for good.* "They started up again four nights ago."

Chad took a deep breath and stared up at the ceiling of the hallway. Bridget nervously jammed her hands deeper into the pockets of her coat. She wouldn't blame him if he stepped back into his apartment and closed the door right in her face. Who in his right mind needed the kind of trouble she was surely bringing? With another deep sigh that seemed to come from the depths of his soul, Chad softly asked, "Why, Bridget? Why me?"

She had to think about which answer to give him. Should she tell him she trusted him? Felt safe with him? How could she burden him with those truths when one simple answer would be enough to stop him from closing the door in her face? Unwanted tears filled her own green eyes as the horror of the vision flashed across her mind.

Brown eyes filled with fear and the knowledge of impending death.

Tears clogged her throat, but she met Chad's gaze steadily as she gave him her answer. "A police officer is going to die." She swallowed the pain those words caused her and gave Chad her fear. "I don't know how to stop it, Chad. I need your help."

Chad closed his eyes as her words registered, but not before she had seen his anguish. Without a word, he moved to the side and opened the door wider. It was an ungracious invitation, but she took it anyway. Beggars couldn't be choosy, and she was definitely a beggar tonight.

Bridget entered the apartment and curiously glanced around. If there was a wife or a significant other in Chad's life, the poor woman needed a crash course in interior decorating. She had seen homier prison cells.

Chad's color theme consisted of one group, brown. The white walls, beige carpeting, brown and beige plaid couch, and brown leather recliner were as bland as oatmeal. A wooden entertainment unit, its doors neatly closed, and the usual assortment of end tables and lamps completed Chad's living room. The only object to break the color theme was a black remote, alone and forgotten on the coffee table.

Chad closed the door behind them. "Make yourself at home. I'll be right back."

As he turned and walked into a short hallway, she stared at his broad shoulders and muscular back. His tan, well-defined back was as devastating as his chest. To safeguard her sanity, the man needed to put on a shirt. For her, temptation usually came in the form of chocolate, not a well-honed male body.

A slow smile teased the corner of her mouth as her gaze slid lower and Chad disappeared into the bedroom. He'd tucked a gun into the back waistband of his jeans. Chad hadn't answered the door unprepared after all. Even when pulled from his bed in the middle of the night, the man was a cop. As long as she could remember that and forget what he looked like half naked, she just might get through the next half hour.

Bridget glanced into the small neat kitchen and sadly shook her head. She wouldn't have thought it possible, but the kitchen was more unadorned than the living room. Not even a used coffee mug littered the counter. Didn't Chad do anything but sleep here?

"Please stop frowning at my kitchen and give me your coat."

She jumped and turned, startled at Chad's voice directly behind her. Her hand flew to cover her pounding heart. "Geez, Barnett, don't you know better than to sneak up on someone like that?"

"Sorry." His hand was outstretched, waiting patiently for her coat. "I didn't mean to startle you, Bridget."

She lowered her hand and started to unbutton her coat. He had pulled on a T-shirt and had zipped and buttoned his jeans, but his feet were still bare and the carpeting appeared thick enough to cover the sound of an approaching elephant. He hadn't meant to unnerve her.

The T-shirt hadn't diminished the temptation one iota. The pale blue material clung to Chad's chest like second skin. Every muscle, ridge, bulge, and valley was outlined lovingly in blue cotton. There wasn't an ounce of fat anywhere. Chad Barnett's body was a menace to polite female society.

Bridget placed her purse on the coffee table and handed Chad her coat. Maybe coming here wasn't such a good idea after all. Maybe she should have called or just dropped him a note. Why was it after five years of trying to respond to a number of nice, safe, good-looking men and failing miserably, her hormones finally woke up to take notice of the one man who would never respond? Hadn't fate dealt her enough blows with the curse?

With a weary sigh, she sank onto the couch and watched as Chad sat in the recliner a good six feet away from her. "I'm sorry for disturbing your sleep, Chad."

"It's okay. Why don't you tell me what you saw?"

Chad knew how it worked. He understood she saw it happen in dreams. Bridget turned away from Chad's probing glance and looked down the hallway toward the partially closed bedroom door. "I'm not going to disturb anyone else's sleep, am I?" The last thing she needed was for Chad's bed partner to overhear her telling him what was going to happen in the future. Some people had a hard time understanding the paranormal.

"I live alone. There's no one here but us."

She refused to dwell on what his living alone meant. She was here for one reason, and one reason only. She needed Chad's help to prevent an officer's death.

Her hands trembled as she clasped them together,

jammed them between her knees, and bowed her head. Where to begin?

"Take your time, Bridget."

"We don't have time. It's going to happen soon. Real soon."

"How is it going to happen? Do you know who? Where?"

She slowly shook her head and her hands gripped each other harder in frustration. She wanted to throw something. Smash something. She wanted to rant and rave at God for cursing her with this *gift*.

"It happens at night. My guess would be deep in the night. Early morning hours. It's been raining, but it must have just stopped. Everything is still wet."

She knew so little. How were they going to stop something of this magnitude with nothing more than fuzzy dreams?

"What's *everything*?"

"An alley. It happens in an alley. There's a couple of rusty dumpsters and chained metal doors. Cinder block and brick walls are covered in graffiti and the ground is littered with trash. The smell of decaying food is heavy in the air."

"You can smell it?"

"Yeah, I can smell rotting food and feel cold, damp air against my skin. The dream has intensified so much over the past four nights that I feared it would happen tonight, but it's not raining outside."

"Have you ever smelled things before?"

"Vaguely. Not enough to really identify anything. This time it's different. This time all of my senses are picking up things."

"All your senses?"

"I can see what's happening. I can hear everything from a dog howling in the distance to a shotgun." She wrapped her arms around herself. She was so cold inside that sometimes she feared she might never be warm again.

"What about taste? What can you taste?"

"The hatred, Chad. It permeates everything. Hatred, danger, and death." She glanced up at him and met his steady gaze. "I wake up with the taste of it in my mouth."

Chad was the first to break eye contact. He ran his hand down his face. "Christ, Bridget." His gaze refused to met hers. Chad seemed to study the wall somewhere over her right shoulder. "How do you stand it?"

"I don't have much choice in the matter." Tears clogged her throat and filled her eyes. She swallowed hard and blinked a few times. "Eventually a person has to sleep no matter how hard they try not to." For her to stop the visions would be like trying to stop breathing. Only death would stop either.

"Cripes, forgive me, Bridget. I shouldn't have said that. I know what those visions do to you."

She nodded. "There's nothing to forgive you for, Chad. You haven't said anything I haven't asked myself a thousand times by now."

"I haven't even offered you something to drink. Would you like a cup of coffee? I could put a pot on."

"No, thank you." The way her nerves were jumping tonight, the last thing she needed was a caffeine fix.

"What about a soda? Beer?"

"Nothing, thank you. I'm fine." It slowly dawned on her Chad was stalling. "Why aren't you asking me what happens in the alley?" The old Chad, the one she knew and trusted, would have been asking questions faster than she could answer.

"Maybe I don't want to know." Chad's voice held a hard edge she had never heard before. "Maybe I don't want to hear how a fellow police officer is gunned down."

"How do you know he's gunned down?"

"You said you could hear a gunshot. I don't need my detective's badge to figure out how he—or is it a she?—dies."

"It's a he." She went back to studying her hands while Chad glared at the blank wall behind her in silence.

It had been a mistake to come here. Grandmom Rosalie said the good Lord only gave a person what they could handle. The Lord had given her the sight so she had no other choice but to handle it. The good Lord hadn't blessed Chad with any gifts. What right did she have to ask him to walk back into hell with her? None whatsoever.

She stood and picked up her purse. "I shouldn't have come, Chad. I'm sorry for disturbing you." She headed for the front door and the coat closet, where Chad had draped her jacket over the doorknob.

"Bridget?"

Her hand froze in midair as she reached for her jacket. She didn't turn to face him because she didn't want him to see the tears in her eyes or the disappointment on her face. She had been counting on him to help her change the future for one man—a man she had never seen before. A man she felt compelled to save. "What?"

"Answer one question before you leave."

She nodded as she pulled her coat off the doorknob.

"What do you expect me to do, Bridget?"

This time she turned to face him. She didn't care if he saw the tears or the disappointment. A man's life was hanging in the balance. "I want you to stop it, Chad."

"Five years ago you asked me to stop it, and I couldn't. You almost died then. What if you're not so lucky this time? What if I get you killed?"

She heard the anguish in his voice and began to realize what the past had cost him. Chad Barnett had been blaming himself for failing her when in fact he'd been the one to save her. She rehung her coat on the knob and returned to the couch.

"Five years ago, Chad, I tried to change the future. I couldn't change it. You couldn't change it. I don't believe anyone could have at the time, but—and this is why I'm here tonight—you stopped it. You stopped the raping and the horrors that plagued my sleep night after endless night. You probably saved countless of other coeds from being beaten and raped that spring. There is no one I trust more."

"How could you trust me?" Chad's voice was loud enough to wake the people in the apartment next door.

"Why shouldn't I? Name one reason."

"Because I failed you." Chad's voice grew louder

with every word. "I should have figured out who it was before he raped you and then nearly killed you."

It didn't get any plainer than that. She had been raped and then nearly choked to death with a lamp cord. Chad had not only arrived on the scene to save her life, he had been wounded in the shoulder and still managed to kill her attacker. His scar had been faintly noticeable earlier and had added another dangerous edge to the appeal of his going shirtless. "You never failed me, Chad. You were there when I needed you the most."

Chad studied her face. He didn't look convinced, but he stopped arguing. With a weary sigh, he ran his hand down his face and then pinched the bridge of his nose. "Tell me what happens in the alley."

"Are you going to help me stop it?" A tiny sprout of hope took root in her heart. With Chad's help, she might be able to change the future. Surely one five-minute slice of time couldn't be that difficult to alter.

"No, Bridget, I'm not going to help you." Chad's frown was as fierce as his glare. "I don't want you anywhere near this. I want you to tell me what happens, and then I will figure out the best way of preventing it."

Chad was going to exclude her. That was fine by her, as long as he was trying to stop it. She'd been in that alley four nights in a row during the visions. She didn't need to be there for the real show. "The only light is coming from a bulb at the far end of the alley. It's windy and the low-wattage light is dangling from a wire. It's swinging back and forth, casting everything into shadows and then light. Everything is in flashes, and it makes it extremely difficult to see accurately."

"What's the first thing you see?"

"The empty alley, and then a man steps into it. His back is toward me. He's wearing dark shoes and pants. He's got short hair. I believe it's dark, too."

"What about a jacket? You said before it was chilly."

"He's wearing a rain poncho that comes to his knees. It's a dark color and there's something written on the back in white letters. I can't read it, though. It's not buttoned, and the wind is twisting it behind him."

"What's he doing?"

"Walking. He's walking to the far end of the alley. He's looking left, then right, then left again. He appears to be searching for something, but I can't be certain. He seems cautious."

"Is he the cop or the killer?"

"The cop."

Chad leaned forward on the recliner. "How do you know he's a cop?"

This was the Chad she remembered. "He reaches the end of the alley, where the light is. A noise startles him."

"What noise?"

"I don't know. It's faint and high-pitched. I can't make it out."

"What's he do?"

"He turns and reaches for his gun. It's in a holster, like you used to wear, under his sports coat." She looked away from Chad and the thousand questions burning in his eyes. "When he first turns, he's in shadows, but then the light swings back. The other night I saw his eyes. They were brown and they held the knowledge he was about to die."

A shudder ripped through her, but she took a deep breath. "Tonight, I purposely didn't look at his face. I watched him reach for his gun, but it didn't clear the holster before the gun blast shattered everything. The momentum of his hand carried the gun out of his holster, but it slipped from his fingers and fell without ever being fired. The wind plastered the poncho to his chest, and on the left breast pocket there was more writing."

A heavy silence filled the room. Chad was the first to break it. "What did the writing say?"

"Philadelphia Police Department."

This time the silence lasted longer. "What happened next?"

"Nothing. The vision ended. The last thing I saw was the writing on the poncho and then nothing but mist."

"Can you remember what the cop looked like? Did he have a mustache or beard? How old did he appear? Full head of hair, or was it receding? Birthmarks, scars—anything, Bridget?"

"Brown eyes. Wide, terror-filled eyes that saw his own death." She stared back down at her trembling hands. "I don't want to look at his face, Chad." Tears slipped silently down her cheeks as she raised her head and pleaded with Chad. "Please don't ask me to look into those eyes again."

TWO

An hour later, Chad thumped the pillow beneath his head and again cursed the too short couch. He had given Bridget his bed. She'd been in no condition to drive herself back home. It was a nice neat reason for her to stay, and she had complied without too much of an argument. He might be able to bend the truth to Bridget, but he couldn't do it to himself. The real reason Bridget was asleep in his bed was for his own peace of mind. Tonight he could keep her safe. Tonight he wouldn't fail her as he had in the past.

Five years, and it still seemed like yesterday's nightmare.

The first time he had seen Bridget, she'd been a twenty-two-year-old senior at one of the city's private colleges. He had been twenty-five, just promoted to detective, full of energy and an ideology that had long since been squashed.

Bridget had stood in front of his desk looking terrified, yet so very brave.

His partner, Frank, had talked to her earlier by phone, and she had agreed to come down to the station to answer some questions. It seemed the week before, Bridget had visited the local precinct and reported a rape was going to take place—a violent, physical rape of a female student at the college she attended.

The officer had scoffed at the notion that she had dreamed the crime, but took down the description anyway. That night the rape had happened exactly as the report claimed it would. The police wanted to know more about her dreams—or what she knew about the rapist.

He hadn't believed in clairvoyance back then, but his partner had been quite anxious to talk to Bridget. After seeing her and hearing her story, Chad still couldn't say he believed in her dreams, but he had been attracted to her. His partner had laughed at the notion of anyone's seeing the future, and they had cleared her of any wrongdoing concerning the crime.

Chad thought the matter had been cleared up concerning Bridget, but the rape was still unsolved. A week later, Bridget was back at his desk. She had dreamed another attack. After a week of dreams, the attack took place—then another and another. Four brutal rapes, where young coeds on her college campus had been unmercifully beaten, occurred before her dreams had changed.

Always before Bridget had dreamed from the attacker's point of view. She saw the young woman's fear and the pitiful attempts to prevent the attack, but she always felt the attacker's hatred and need.

It was as though she had been inside the attacker's mind at the time of the attacks.

But she began to dream she was the victim, the one being raped and beaten by a man wearing a ski mask.

Chad hadn't liked the change in her dreams, so he took her off the campus and moved her into a nearby apartment. His partner wasn't convinced she was seeing the future, but was acting leery of her.

Chad had believed her. He had seen what the visions were doing to her. Bridget looked at him with trust and hope shining in her honest green eyes. He was her only hope of stopping the dreams by catching the serial rapist. He would have done anything to earn that trust.

The dreams had continued for a week, and Bridget had been near the breaking point. She was terrified of sleeping. He and his partner visited her before staking out the campus with every available policeman the city could spare. Concerned for her health, they had gotten a doctor to prescribe some sleeping pills for her. They had left her apartment with a guard posted in the living room and Bridget comfortably settled in the bedroom.

He had been staking out the campus for about two hours when something began to feel wrong. First he couldn't locate his partner. Then he'd started thinking about his partner's recent behavior. Something wasn't right.

He knew he was the junior partner and should be following his senior partner's lead, but two plus two were not adding up to four. He had used his radio to contact the guard in Bridget's apartment and had gotten no response.

Panic stricken and full of dread, he had raced to the nearby apartment. The sound of glass breaking in Bridget's bedroom reached his ears as he raced up the stairs. The guard was unconscious on the living-room floor. He could remember only his need to reach Bridget, to make sure she was safe.

With one powerful kick, he shattered the bedroom door and faced a sight that had plagued his sleep ever since.

Bridget had been pinned to the bed by the rapist. An electrical cord had been wrapped around her neck and the rapist was choking the life out of her. The attacker turned. In the light filtering through the doorway, he had seen it was his partner, Frank.

A fleeting moment of surprise slowed his response time down, and Frank reached for his gun and fired first. The bullet struck Chad's left shoulder, but he had still managed to get off a shot. His shot had been true, and Frank had been dead before he tumbled off the bed.

Chad had rushed to Bridget. Though horribly beaten and raped, she had been alive. He had a vague recollection of radioing for help as he cradled her broken body and prayed. The last time he'd seen her, they had been loading her into an ambulance.

The Internal Affairs investigation into the rapes and the killing of his partner had been mercifully swift. Bridget didn't have to appear in any court-room, and the story was swept pretty much under the carpet. The powers-that-be at police headquarters didn't want it known a clairvoyant had been helping the police to capture a serial rapist and had somehow managed to become a victim. They figured if she was that clairvoyant, she should have known who the attacker was in the first place. Surely she could have saved herself.

He had known differently.

He knew how much she had suffered through every one of those visions. He also knew he had failed her. He should have been the one to see the signs that the serial rapist had been his own partner, should have been the one to protect her. He had the training and the detective's shield, not Bridget.

He should have realized when her dreams changed she was going to become the victim and taken better precautions. The one guard had been easily drugged by Frank with Bridget's own sleeping pills.

While Bridget had been in the hospital, he couldn't bear to visit her and see that the trust had died from her gorgeous green eyes, eyes that had haunted him for five years. To see her would be like confronting his own failures head on. He had sent her flowers instead. Whatever attraction he had first felt for Bridget back then had been buried under an avalanche of guilt. He had done the only honorable thing he knew. He had gotten out of her life and stayed out.

What future could they have had, anyway? Every time Bridget looked at him, she'd remember the past. He couldn't do that to her.

After five long years, Bridget was back in his life

and a fellow officer was in danger. What the hell was he supposed to do? She had come to him for help. If he pushed her away, he would fail her once again. But if he tried to help her only to fail once again, what would it do not only to her but to him? How would he live with himself if he failed Bridget twice?

With a frustrated groan, he kicked the arm of the couch and tried to find a more comfortable position. After several minutes of forcing his mind to go blank and his body to relax, he fell into a light, dreamless sleep.

An hour later, his sleep and his peace of mind were severely shaken by Bridget's terror-filled scream. He rushed to the bedroom door, gun drawn, and took his first breath since waking when he saw Bridget was alone in bed. His trained eyes scanned the room for an intruder, but he knew he wouldn't find one. What had frightened her he was powerless to protect her from. He slowly put the safety back on the gun and placed it on the bureau before approaching the bed.

In the low light from the hall, he saw Bridget was curled up on her side and she was covering her head with her arms, a pitiful attempt to ward off more of the vision. He could tell she was awake by the slight rhythmic rocking of her body. He had seen small children use the same defense mechanisms when the world and all its horrors threatened to overcome them.

Cautiously, so as not to startle her, he sat on the edge of the bed and stared at the arch of her back. She hadn't undressed or even gotten under the covers. Bridget was still wearing the sweatshirt and jeans she had arrived in. It was a smart move. A woman should never take off her clothes when using a stranger's bed, even if the stranger was a cop and she had known him five years earlier. People change. It would have been asking for trouble.

"It's me, Bridget." He reached out and gently touched her shoulder. Her gray sweatshirt was soft and warm beneath his hand, but it didn't stop him from feeling the tremors shaking her body. "Are you okay?"

Bridget slowly nodded and relaxed her arms, but didn't turn to face him. She pressed her face deeper into his pillow.

"Was it the same dream?" He knew it would be, but he felt compelled to ask. In the past he had never been there when she'd had a dream, but had seen the damage they had caused in the morning light. Tonight he was going to experience the damage first-hand.

Again she nodded, and her arms hugged the pillow, her voice barely a whisper. "I stayed with it as long as I could."

He involuntarily gripped her shoulder harder. He didn't want to think what her determination to stay within the vision had cost her.

"Do you want to talk about it?" The professional inside him wanted a full account now, while it was still fresh in her mind. The man inside him wanted her to wait until morning or even next week, when it might not be as painful to talk about.

Bridget turned and looked up at him. Tears were

running down her pale cheeks, and her green eyes swam with more. The man inside him won.

Without thought, he reached down and pulled her up against his chest. His arms tightened around her as she clung to him and cried. Warm tears soaked the T-shirt he had pulled on after her arrival, but he didn't try to stop her. Bridget needed this emotional release. If he wasn't mistaken, she had just witnessed a man being shot right in front of her.

He'd learned before when Bridget experienced one of her visions, it was like she was right there. They were as real to her as if they had just happened.

When her tears started to slow and the sobs racking her body eased, he reached for a fistful of tissues from the nightstand and pushed them into her hand. He was way out of his league here, and he knew it. Holding a crying woman was as foreign to him as cradling a newborn baby. A baby he could hand back to its mother or someone else. What in the world was he supposed to do with a crying woman—and in his bed, no less?

Bridget took the tissues, muttered a watery thanks, and then moved out of his arms. She blew her nose and wiped her eyes as she swung her legs over the side of the bed and sat next to him.

Her first words shocked the breath right out of him. "It's a game."

"What's a game?"

"I don't know." Bridget's eyes silently begged him to understand. "The killer didn't say anything, but it's like I can read his mind. His thoughts are thrown out into the air, into the very air that surrounds me.

He killed the right man, but not the real victim. It's a game to him, one he's very determined to win."

"You say he. Is the killer a man?"

Bridget got as far as "Ye . . ." before closing her mouth. In the dim room, he couldn't see her eyes, but he knew she was thinking and thinking hard.

"I don't know, Chad. I want to say yes, but that might be because I could never envision a woman firing that gun and taking a life so heartlessly. To me, a cold-blooded killer like this has to be a man. Nothing in the vision gave me proof one way or another." She wiped at her eyes again. "I guess it could be a woman."

He reached out and squeezed her trembling hand. "It's okay, Bridget. You're right in your thinking. Most killers are men."

Bridget studied their clasped hands for a moment before continuing. "I figured out what the sound was that startled the officer into turning around and trying to draw his gun."

"What?"

"A chuckle. An eerie, off-center, rough chuckle." A shudder ripped through her body and she pressed her other hand over their already clasped hands. "I can't tell if it came from a woman or a man."

How could it get worse? A chuckle? What kind of sick individual were they dealing with? One who would kill a cop in cold blood, obviously. "What do you mean by off center?"

"I don't know. It was off key and uncontrolled, like the person hadn't meant to do it, but it just came out and surprised them both."

"Could there have been anyone else in the alley besides the killer and the officer?"

"No, there were only two people in the alley and the laugh came from the killer." Bridget squeezed his hand so tight he almost cringed, but she wouldn't meet his gaze. "The killer chuckled another time."

"When?"

"After shooting the officer. While he was crumpling to the ground." Bridget studied the carpet at their feet. "The officer has short brown hair. No receding hairline or bald spots I could detect. No gray, either. Eyebrows a little on the bushy side. His ears were normal, not too big or small."

"What about his nose? Mouth? Anything else?" Bridget had just described nearly half the force. He needed more information, a better description, *anything* if he was to find this particular needle in the haystack.

"I didn't get that far. The bullet entered his forehead, right above his left eye." Bridget cleared her throat twice before she could continue. "The impact forced his head to snap back and his arm to fly up into the air. That's when he lost the gun he'd been reaching for."

He pulled her closer and wrapped an arm around her shoulder. "You don't have to continue, Bridget. I can fill in the blanks." He heard the horror and the tears in her voice and it tore at his heart. No one should have to describe such a scene.

"The brick wall behind him is splattered with blood and pieces of his brain." Uncontrollable sobs racked her body as he pulled her into his arms.

"Shhh . . . Bridget, it's okay. Don't say any more. Don't remember anything else." This gentle woman in his arms wasn't prepared or equipped to handle this dark and ugly side of life. Hell, he barely managed to keep his own stomach under control when he arrived on the scene of a homicide. Many a good officer had lost his dinner at more than one scene.

"Rocco." Bridget buried her face against his chest and muttered the word once again. "Rocco Rules."

"Rocco rules what? Who's Rocco?"

"I don't know. It was spray painted on the wall behind the officer. It's splattered with blood and gore now." This time there was no stopping the tears or her tearful plea. It went straight to his heart. "Make it stop, Chad. Please, make it all go away."

In one swift movement, he lifted her up and placed her on his lap. His arms tightened around her, and he slowly rocked her back and forth as if giving comfort to a small child. He knew he had lost the battle with himself when she rested her head on his shoulder and relaxed in his arms. It was as if she had done it a thousand times in the past. "I can only promise I'll try, Bridget."

A weary sigh escaped the depths of his soul as his gaze traveled to his window and the darkness beyond. At least it wasn't raining. The killing wouldn't happen tonight. Tonight he wouldn't fail her. "All I can promise is that I'll try."

Bridget stayed in the comfort of Chad's arms for a long time. She needed this physical contact with another human being, a warm, caring human being.

It had been so long since anyone had held her, really held her—five years, to be precise.

Ever since what she thought of as the incident, she had shied away from close physical contact with anyone outside her immediate family. She still hugged her parents, her brothers, and Grandmom Rosalie, but that was about it. The few dates she had gone on went well, and she had even enjoyed herself on a few occasions, until the relationship processed to the next logical point—physical contact.

As soon as one of her dates pulled her into his arms, even for something as natural and unthreatening as a light good-night kiss, panic froze her and uncontrollable terror filled her mind. A man's physical strength over her terrified her to the point of avoiding all physical contact with men.

So why did she feel so safe in Chad's arms? She should be backing off faster than a Maryland crab. Instead, she pressed closer to his warmth and strength. There was no denying Chad's strength. It was in his arms, the broadness of his shoulders, and the hardness of his chest. It was a gentle strength that could turn deadly in an instant. He had been trained to use that strength. So why did she feel so protected?

Contradictions. Once again, Chad was full of contradictions she didn't understand. One of his large, warm hands was rubbing her back and he was muttering gentle soothing words into her hair. She wished she could hear the words, but his voice was soft and soothing. It was enough for now.

She closed her eyes and allowed Chad to hold her

world together for the next few moments as she did nothing more than concentrate on the steady warmth of his hand rubbing her back and the enticing scent filling her head. Shampoo, soap, and the male scent of Chad were such a break from the floral fragrances she was used to that they pulled at her senses and begged to be appreciated.

Chad shifted. "Are you feeling better now?"

His sudden movement surprised her. "What?"

"I asked if you were feeling better now."

Bridget took in their positions and nearly groaned in mortification. She was on Chad's lap, on his bed, and wrapped around him. When she decided to lose her inhibitions, she just didn't drop them, she burned them. "Oh, Lord, I'm sorry." She shuffled off his lap so fast she would have fallen to the floor if Chad hadn't caught her.

"Easy, Bridget." He steadied her and then stood up. "How about if I go put on a pot of coffee? It's nearly dawn and I don't think either one of us will be getting any more sleep tonight."

"Sounds good." She brushed a lock of her hair away from her face and grimaced at the dampness her tears had caused. "Could I use your bathroom to freshen up?"

Chad nodded toward the hallway. "It's right outside the door. Help yourself."

"Thanks." She hurried out the doorway and into the bathroom. The fluorescent bulb above the medicine cabinet mirror was a cruel jolt of reality. The bright light was unforgiving, and she had a lot that needed forgiving tonight. Her eyes were swollen from crying, her nose would have done Rudolph proud, and whatever color she had left in her face the unmerciful light bleached right out. She looked like an extra on the set of the movie "The Night of the Living Dead." Heck, she looked like the star. It would be a miracle if Chad didn't suffer from nightmares after tonight.

A small cabinet revealed neatly folded linen, and she helped herself to a beige washcloth. She soaked it in cold water and pressed it to her face and eyes. The ravages of four sleepless nights weren't going anywhere, but hopefully by the time she faced Chad in the kitchen she would appear semihuman again.

What the hell had she been thinking? Sitting on Chad's lap, crying in his arms, and then smelling him! Maybe that was the problem. She hadn't been thinking at all. For the first time in five years, she had reacted to a man with an emotion that wasn't terror.

She slowly pulled the washcloth away from her face and stared into the mirror. The woman staring back at her was the one who had always been there. The exhaustion and the recent round of tears were still in evidence, but she was the same. Nothing glamorous, but nothing repulsive.

The bright red hair she had been born with had calmed down to what she liked to consider auburn. In reality, it still held too many red highlights, but it was close. Her nose was okay, but her mouth was too big. Her eyes were a light green when she would have preferred a rich, dark emerald green. The freckles that had plagued her as a child had faded with time, but still were too numerous for her liking. Her complexion was clear, but entirely too pale, partly from exhaustion, but mostly because she suffered the same fate as most natural redheads. If she went out into the sun, she was guaranteed to burn.

She neatly folded the washcloth and placed it on the edge of the sink.

What in the world was she looking at? She knew what she looked like. She hadn't changed magically because she finally didn't cringe when a man held her. It didn't mean anything. Chad had been as unthreatening as any one of her brothers would have been if they had been holding her. Chad hadn't been holding her with desire. He had been offering comfort, nothing more.

She took a deep breath, straightened her shoulders, and finger combed her hair the best she could. Her purse was still on the coffee table and she wasn't vain enough to rummage through it to locate a comb. Chad would just have to suffer.

Again she slid her fingers through her hair to comb it back from her face but failed. They slowly slid down her throat to the thin white scar encircling it, clearly visible above the neckline of her sweatshirt.

For three years after the incident, she had worn high-necked blouses, turtlenecks and even scarves to hide the mark. One day she realized she hadn't been hiding it at all. It didn't matter what other people thought of it. People generally thought what they wanted to think, and there wasn't a darn thing she could say or do to change their minds. It was what she thought that mattered. If she allowed the sight of it to remind her of that horrible night, then Frank Barelli had won and continued to win even after his death.

She couldn't allow that to continue, so she had stopped hiding behind high-necked clothes. Most people when they first noticed it were curious, but were too well-mannered to ask about it.

Chad, on the other hand, knew all about it. He had witnessed firsthand who and what had caused the mark. It was their past, and neither of them could change it now. Why dwell on it? She wasn't here to change the past, only the future.

With a weary sigh and a prayer that they could change the future for one man, she left the bathroom and headed for the kitchen.

Chad dumped a pot of water into the coffeemaker and cursed as his trembling fingers spilled more than a few drops down the side of the machine. What was wrong with him?

He heard the water running in the bathroom and knew his answer. Bridget and her haunting green eyes were what was wrong. One minute he was holding her and comforting her from her latest tears. The next he was practically shoving her off his lap before he felt something he had no business feeling.

Desire, thick and heavy, had pooled in his groin. For one blinding moment in the bedroom, he had wanted Bridget Mackenzie with such intensity it had scared him spitless. He'd never felt such raging desire in his life.

The poor woman had just gone through a terrifying experience and was counting on his help, and all he could think about was kissing her. What kind of man did that make him?

Most men would probably tell him it was a normal reaction to having a beautiful woman sitting on his lap on a welcoming and warm bed. He wasn't most men. He felt like a lecher. He knew better than to get emotionally involved in any case he was working on. He knew it was one of the cardinal rules of being a good cop.

Emotions screwed you up. They got in the way of your thinking and eventually would cause you to make an error in your judgment. He knew this as well as he knew his own name. Experience had taught him well.

Five years ago, his attraction for Bridget had gotten in the way of the case. Maybe if he had stopped thinking about her all the time, he would have concentrated more on his partner, Frank, and put it all together before that fateful night.

He carefully measured out the coffee and started the machine. He wasn't going to let his emotions get involved this time. He owed Bridget his best. He had promised her his help. That meant he had to concentrate fully on the case, not go off on some fanciful daydream of getting Bridget in his bed, naked and under him. He needed to get himself and his wayward hormones under control.

He reached for two coffee mugs, placed them on the counter, and then shut the cabinet door a little harder than necessary. It didn't make him feel any better.

"Are you all right?"

He turned and saw Bridget standing there looking at him funny. He didn't blame her. "I'm fine. Just a little tired." He reached for the sugar bowl that was in another cabinet.

"Sorry, that's my fault."

"I'm not due on until eleven tonight. I'll catch a nap later. What about you?" He poured the coffee into the cups and handed her one. "Cream?"

"Please." Bridget stirred in a spoonful of sugar. "It will be a long day. We're open until eight."

He reached in the refrigerator and took out the carton of milk. "Milk okay?"

"Fine." Bridget poured the milk and handed him back the carton. "Thanks."

"Where are you working?" Last he knew, Bridget hadn't been sure which direction in life she wanted to follow once she graduated from college. She had been taking a variety of business courses. He put the milk away and headed for the recliner in the other room. The kitchen was too small for both of them. He needed more space.

"It's a little flower shop on South Hampton Road in the northeast. It's called The Garden of Eden. Ever hear of it?"

"No, I don't get up to the northeast section very often. I mainly work in Center City." He sat in the recliner and watched as Bridget gracefully lowered herself onto the sofa. Bridget worked with flowers. He never would have pictured that, but it seemed right somehow. "So do you like arranging flowers?" He didn't know anyone who actually worked in a flower shop, but he assumed that was what one did there.

"I'd better." Bridget took a sip of coffee and gave him a small smile. "I own the shop."

"You own your own business?"

"Lock, stock, and a ten-year lease." Bridget took another drink before placing the cup on the coffee table. "Why so shocked?"

"I'm not shocked, just startled. I've never known anyone who actually owned a business."

He knew Tony down the street who owned the pizza parlor, but it wasn't the same. Tony was just an acquaintance and a man who made one hell of a pizza. A couple of cops talked about getting their own place when their magic numbers for retirement rolled around. Vinnie wanted to open up a liquor store and Rancowski wanted a pet shop. Phil talked about opening a bait shop in Montana, but since Phil had never been to Montana or even fishing, Chad figured he was all talk and no action.

"I hear owning your own business is a real hassle when it comes to paperwork and the government."

"Why do you think I took all those business courses?"

"I guess that would help."

"That and a good accountant. I can tell you horror stories on the amount of paperwork required for one little shop. It takes half a Ponderosa pine to appease the I.R.S. and the other half to appease the state and city." Bridget gave him another little smile. "I wouldn't have it any other way, though."

He couldn't take his eyes off that small, nearly unnoticeable smile. The slight curving of her lips and a certain gleam in her eyes made him catch his breath and wait for more. A full-blown smile from her would probably be blinding.

In all the time he'd known her, Bridget had rarely had anything to smile about. Right this moment, it was different. She wasn't thinking about the visions that haunted her or the past. She was talking about her business.

"What's your favorite part of the business? What do you like doing the most?"

"Arranging the flowers and working with the small inventory of plants I carry. I don't care for silk flowers, but they're a necessary part of the business. I love the smell and texture of real flowers."

"What's the worst part?"

"The paperwork. Piles and piles of paperwork from ordering in merchandise to receiving to paying the bills. It's unending and thankless. There's payroll and more taxes than I could name if someone paid me a thousand dollars." Bridget picked up her cup and drank some more.

He finished his coffee and put the empty cup on the table beside him. "Don't you have a computer?"

"Two. One at the shop and one at home. I do a lot of the paperwork at home. It frees me up for the things I like to do when I'm at the shop."

"It must make for some long days." When did she find time for a social life? A quick glance at her left hand confirmed what he had already suspected—no wedding band, no engagement ring.

"No one ever said owning my own business would be easy." Bridget finished her coffee. The small, hesitant smile was gone.

"I imagine it's not." He wanted to see that smile one more time. Without thinking, he asked the first question that popped into his mind. "What's your favorite flower?"

"Daisies. It's still daisies, Chad."

He knew that. He closed his eyes and cursed himself for being such a fool. Five years ago he had known daisies were her favorite flower—had even sent her an entire bouquet of them when she was in the hospital. "I'm sorry, Bridget. I wasn't thinking."

"It's okay, Chad. We can't tiptoe around the past."

He felt worse. Not only had he brought up the past, he had taken away what little joy she had found by talking about her flower shop. He glanced at her empty cup. "Would you like another cup of coffee? There's plenty left."

"No, thank you. I should be going." Bridget looked out the patio doors leading to his miniature balcony. "It's morning and the boogey man has disappeared with the darkness." Bridget stood up and carried her cup into the kitchen.

He followed with his and put them both in the sink for later. "Give me a second and I'll walk you to your car."

"I'm a big girl, Chad. You don't have to walk me to the parking lot."

"We need to discuss a few more things." He left

her standing there putting on her shoes and headed for his bedroom and the old pair of sneakers lying in his closet. A minute later, jamming his arms into a jacket, he joined her by the front door.

Bridget preceded him into the hallway and headed for the steps. "What is there to talk about?"

"First, there's a few conditions on my agreement to help you."

"Such as?"

He kept pace with her as they descended the stairs. "I don't want you involved."

Bridget came to a complete standstill and stared at him. "That's going to be a little hard to do."

"I know." He was sounding unrealistic, but he didn't know what else to do. "I want you as far away from this as possible. I don't want anyone to know about you, your name, or your visions."

Bridget couldn't hide the hurt in her eyes. "Because I'm a clairvoyant?"

He reached out and gently touched her cheek. "No. Because you might get hurt. I won't risk that again, Bridget." Her skin felt like warm silk beneath his fingertips.

"How can you help me if I'm not allowed to be involved? I have to give you clues from the visions. I'm the only lead."

"I don't know yet. Give me today to think about it, okay? I'll call you tomorrow morning when I'm done with my shift." He lowered his hand and jammed it into the pocket of his jacket before he gave in to the temptation to do more than just touch her cheek. "Maybe I can borrow one of those computer programs that lets you compile a suspect's face on the screen and then prints it out. We can try to do one of the cop."

"I didn't see that much of his face, Chad."

He saw the frustration in her eyes and gave her both hope and a curse. "Maybe tonight you will."

Bridget turned away and started down the steps once again. "Yeah, tonight."

His hand grabbed her arm and made her stop. "You don't have to do it, Bridget, if you don't want to."

"You don't understand, Chad." Bridget's voice rose to a near shout. "I can't stop it!" She pulled her arm out of his grip and continued down the stairs and out the door.

What the hell was he supposed to say to that? He hadn't been the one to go banging on her door at nearly one o'clock in the morning. He hadn't been the one to cost her a night's sleep or to beg her to help him.

He followed along quietly until she reached the same car she'd been driving five years earlier. It looked exactly the same. He stood there as she unlocked it and opened the door. Even at this early hour, a garbage truck was rumbling its way through the neighborhood, banging cans and making dogs bark.

Bridget nervously jiggled her keys. "I shouldn't have yelled at you like that. None of this is your fault. I'm a little tired and cranky right now."

"After the night you just had, it's understandable, Bridget. You don't have to apologize."

"Will you still help?"

"As much as I can."

Bridget opened her purse and, after some searching, pulled out a business card and a pen. She quickly wrote a number on the back of the card and handed it to him. "This is my home phone number and the shop's. If I'm not at one, I'll be at the other."

"I'll call tomorrow morning, okay?" Maybe by then he would be able to figure out how to locate the cop to make sure he didn't go into any alleys at night and how to keep Bridget out of it all. A man couldn't have all this dumped on him and be expected to come up with a plan within a couple of hours. It took some thinking time. Good quality thinking time.

Bridget got into the car. "Chad?"

His hands were on the door, ready to shut it. "Yeah?"

"Thanks."

Those soft green eyes once again touched his heart. Bridget Mackenzie was one dangerous woman. "You're welcome. Now drive safely." He shut her door before she could cause more damage to his control.

He stepped back and watched as she drove out of the parking lot and down the street. With a heavy sigh, he turned and walked back into the building. He never noticed the dark blue sedan parked across the street or its occupant watching every move he made.

THREE

Bridget turned on the cold water faucet with a trembling hand. Cupping both hands beneath the running water, she took a deep breath, lowered her head, and splashed. The freezing water from the bathroom sink hit her flushed face and sucked the air right out of her lungs. Wakefulness returned with a jolt, as she had been praying it would. She needed to think, and she needed a clear head to do it.

Tonight, just as Chad had hoped, the dream had returned and she'd gotten a better look at the cop's face. He was older than Chad by a few years; she'd guess midthirties. His nose was on the big side, but Cyrano wouldn't have to worry about competition. A dark, thick, and bushy mustache rested beneath that nose. Tonight she had stayed with the vision longer, and it hadn't been the noise of the fatal gun blast that wakened her. It had been something worse, much worse. A thunderclap and lightning from outside her own bedroom window had pulled her from her sleep. It was storming outside.

She had to tell Chad!

She splashed another handful of water onto her

face and reached for a towel. What was she thinking? It was one in the morning. Chad had probably realized it was raining the minute the first raindrop splattered on his windshield. While she had been snuggled all warm in her bed, Chad had been at work for a good two hours.

Still clutching the towel, she hurried downstairs, past the mess of ladders and the drop cloths cluttering her living room, and into the kitchen. French patio doors opened to the backyard and brought all the weather into the bright yellow and white room. At this hour, only darkness and the occasional flash of lightning flooded the room. She flipped on the light switch and went to stand before the doors.

Rain was pouring down and the wind was ripping leaves from the trees. With the onset of chillier weather, the leaves had been changing colors for the past two weeks. The brilliant display of color was gone. Tonight everything appeared dark, dismal, and dangerous. Tonight the vision could come true.

She pressed her forehead against the cold glass of the door. Wet leaves tumbled across the slate patio only to end up plastered against whatever they touched. A shiver slid down her spine as a puddle formed in a low spot. Puddles had been in the alley. She had to tell Chad she had seen the policeman's face. But what good would it do? Chad was working and wouldn't be free until the morning. What good would it do if he learned the officer was in his midthirties and had a big nose and bushy mustache? How was he to locate such a man out of thousands?

The officer would be safe as long as it was raining. In the vision, the rain had already stopped.

Quickly, as the idea came to her, she ran to the television and turned it on. She jabbed in the numbers for The Weather Channel and cursed as some smiling woman in a red suit and matching lipstick told her about a low pressure system over Detroit. She didn't care what kind of weather Detroit was having. She wanted Philadelphia's forecast.

A minute later the local report filled the screen and she relaxed. The storm was expected to last all night and into the morning rush hour. It would be raining all night long. The bad news was that tomorrow night another storm would move through. Chad would have to work fast to discover the identity of the officer in time.

She watched the rest of the local report and then went back into the kitchen to make herself a cup of tea. A nice cup of hot herbal tea and some obscure old movie was just the thing to make her sleepy again. Tomorrow morning, with its million and one things to do, would arrive soon enough.

Shamrock, her cat and the real boss around the house, joined her as the kettle started to whistle. "There you are, Shammy. I was wondering where you were." She picked up the black cat rubbing itself against her leg and gave the feline a loving scratch behind its ears. Shamrock was entirely black, with just the tip of her tail dipped in white. Her gold eyes seemed to look down on the world around her. "Did I disturb your beauty sleep?"

Shamrock moved her head so Bridget could reach under her chin, then gave a soft meow.

Bridget complied with the not-so-subtle request. "I'm sorry, baby. I know the last couple of nights haven't been easy on you, either, what with me up and wandering the house at all hours of the night and then not even coming home last night. I hope I didn't worry you too much." It had been the first time she'd left Shamrock alone all night long, and she felt guilty about it.

The cat nudged Bridget's fingers with the top of its head and purred. "Yeah, I hear you." She gave Shamrock another scratch and then put her down. While the tea brewed, she got Shamrock a couple of kitty snacks and placed them on the floor. "That's all you get for tonight, old gal. You already had your dinner. If I keep feeding you treats, you'll be waddling around this old place like an overfed goose." She gave Shamrock one last scratch. "Believe me, there's nothing worse than a waddling cat."

Shamrock downed the first treat without even chewing it and gave a belligerent meow. Bridget chuckled and carried her tea into the other room. "Just you wait and see. You keep eating like that, and that old tomcat from next door won't be howling at the patio door come spring."

She sat down on the couch, pulled the afghan Grandmom Rosalie had crocheted for her over her bare legs, and flipped through the channels. Within minutes, the tea was finished and she was lying on the couch with Shamrock curled up behind her knees. The pounding rain, crashing thunder, and bolts of lightning splitting the night sky outside the window gave her comfort. An old John Wayne western was playing softly on the television. She never even knew which movie it was. She was asleep before the three remaining drops of tea in the bottom of her cup had cooled.

A loud pounding at the front door woke her from the first restful sleep she'd had in nearly a week. The television was showing some muscle-bound grinning idiot doing situps and begging her not to give up yet. John Wayne had obviously ridden off into the sunset. The rain was still coming down, but she didn't hear any thunder. The morning skies beyond the window looked dark and dismal. It was the perfect morning to pull the covers up over her head and sleep in. Now if whoever was pounding on her door would just go away, she could catch another hour or so of sleep before heading to work.

Another round of pounding got her up off the couch. She wrapped the afghan around her shoulders and glared at Shamrock. The cat wriggled her way into the warm indentation Bridget had left. "Don't get too comfortable. I'll be right back."

Bridget glanced out the front window and saw a relatively new sports utility vehicle parked behind her vintage Saturn. Her parents and grandmother had bought her the car brand new as a high school graduation and going away to college gift. She didn't recognize the S.U.V., and from this angle she couldn't see who was pounding on her door. She drew the afghan closer and, making sure the chain was on the door, she cracked it open.

Chad stood there staring back at her—a very wet, different looking Chad. Something had happened. Something bad. She quickly closed the door, released the chain, and reopened the door so he could come in. "Chad, what's wrong?"

Chad stepped into the house and closed the door behind him. The look he gave her was both frightening and full of pain. "It happened, Bridget. Just like you said it would."

She glanced out the window and shook her head. "No, it didn't. It couldn't have. It's still raining." She continued to shake her head. This wasn't happening. She refused to believe she had been wrong. "It hasn't stopped raining all night."

Chad brushed back a lock of hair that had fallen onto his forehead and, with the sleeve of his soaked jacket, wiped at the few drops of water still running down his face. "There was a break in the storm around one. It lasted five minutes or so. That's all it took."

Around one o'clock! She had been having the vision as the murder had been taking place. She closed her eyes and silently apologized to the slain officer. She hadn't been fast enough to save his life. Why had God cursed her with this gift if she was never to be in time to save anyone? She looked at Chad and her heart nearly broke in two. He appeared to be in shock. "Did you know the officer?"

Chad looked at her for a long moment before softly answering, "He was my partner."

"Oh, God, Chad. I'm sorry." She wanted to pull him into her arms and offer him the same comfort he had offered her last night. Chad didn't look like he would be too receptive to that idea. He looked like he wanted to smash, break, or destroy something. She didn't blame him. To lose his partner like that would have been horrible enough, but to know before it would happen was worse. Much worse. She reached out and touched his arm. "What can I do?"

"Do? What do you mean, what can you do?" Chad's voice rose, and for the first time she heard the anger behind his pain. "Haven't you done enough?"

She understood both his anger and his pain. He needed to vent them both, and she was the only one here. "It's never enough, Chad. I'm sorry I didn't have all the answers. I'm sorry we couldn't have stopped it."

"Why, Bridget? Why did you see *this* crime out of a city full of crime?" Chad thrust his fingers through his hair and droplets of water scattered everywhere. "Why after five years did your visions start again, and why are they always connected to me?"

She shook her head. Hadn't she asked herself those same questions for days now? "I don't know." It seemed inadequate, but she didn't know what else to tell him. "Give me your jacket. You're soaking wet. Have you been outside all night in that rain?"

"Just about." Chad unzipped the windbreaker that had been useless against the elements outside and handed it to her.

Bridget quickly read the label on the inside—tumble dry. Chad's sweatshirt and wet jeans needed a good half hour in the dryer, too. "I know this is going to sound strange, but take off your shirt and jeans and I'll toss everything into the dryer."

Without waiting for his response, she headed for the hall closet and pulled out a spare blanket she kept there. "Wrap this around you to keep warm. Make sure everything's out of your pockets."

When he continued to stand there and stare at her as if she had lost her mind, she added, "The last thing you need now is a cold. You have a killer to catch, not pneumonia."

"How do you know I'm going after the killer?"

"You wouldn't be here if you weren't. You want more information, and you won't get it from me until your clothes are drying." She shoved the blanket into his hands and turned around as if the problem were solved.

"Powder room is there." She nodded her head in the direction of the room. "I'll wait in the kitchen."

Chad stood there for a moment holding the blanket and staring down the short hall into the kitchen. Mark Monterey, his partner for the last five years, was dead, and Bridget wanted his clothes. When was this night going to end?

He glanced at his watch. It was seven forty-six in the morning. The night was over, but it only continued into a hellish day. Bridget was right. He did want information. He was going to catch Mark's killer if it was the last thing he did. He'd parade around bare-ass naked to get a lead, any lead. What the police had now was absolutely nothing. Whatever evidence might have been left in the alley was gone. The torrential rain that had been falling all night had washed everything away.

He headed for the bathroom and for the first time noticed the room he had been standing in. He assumed it was the living room, or one day would be a living room. Now it was a large room filled with ladders, drop cloths, and paint cans. Most of the sheet rock on the walls was new. Someone was investing a lot of time, money, and effort into redoing the room. Those were the main reasons he was still living in an apartment.

The small but adequate powder room had obviously just been redone, and by a woman's hand. The damned room sparkled and gleamed with white porcelain, brass fixtures, and a gilded mirror that covered the entire wall above the sink. The walls were painted a pale green, but someone had stenciled trailing ivy everywhere. Even the hand towels hanging from shining brass rings had embroidered ivy trailing down them. He pulled the damp sweatshirt over his head and placed it on the edge of the antique white pedestal sink.

A rectangular stained glass window was placed high enough for privacy and would have let in plenty of light if the sun had been shining. He dug into his pockets and pulled out the contents. He had to move a glass bowl of potpourri and a wooden birdhouse to make room on the back of the toilet. The raspberry potpourri was making his nose itch.

He kicked off his soaked sneakers, socks, and jeans. He'd gone to work in his normal khakis and shirt with a sports jacket. It wasn't cold enough yet for a heavier jacket. When he had reached Mark, he could do nothing but cradle his lifeless body and stare at the graffiti on the blood-splattered wall. *Rocco Rules!* It had been just as Bridget had predicted, right down to good old Rocco.

He had cleaned up and changed into a spare set of clothes he had in his car down at the precinct, then insisted on accompanying the commissioner to tell Mark's wife she was now a widow. It was the hardest thing he'd ever done.

He had promised Cindy Monterey he would catch her husband's killer. To do that he needed some help, and Bridget was the only player holding any cards. He wrapped the blanket around his shoulders, picked up his damp clothes, and headed for the kitchen.

Bridget had a pot of coffee already brewing by the time he stepped into the bright and cheery room. One thing he had noticed since entering her home was that the woman loved color. It was enough to blind a man. He handed her the damp clothes without saying a word and she disappeared down a flight of steps to the basement.

He was standing in front of the patio doors watching the rain when she came back into the room. He didn't bother to turn around. "His name was Mark Monterey."

Referring to Mark in the past tense was hard. He still couldn't believe he was gone. Just like that! In the time it had taken him to get a cup of coffee, his partner's life was over.

Tears clogged his throat, and he had to swallow twice before continuing. "Mark was honest, hard-working, and too compassionate for the job. He'd been a sucker for every hard-luck story that came our way. Believe me, there were plenty over the years."

He couldn't count the times he'd had to buy Mark's lunch because his partner had given away all the money Cindy had handed him that morning. Cindy had learned early in their marriage to allow Mark only so much money, or it would all disappear, given to some hard-luck case.

"He had a wife and two small girls at home." He couldn't see the rain anymore because of the tears. He tried blinking them away, but they wouldn't go. He knew eventually they would come, but he didn't want Bridget to see them, to see his weakness. To him, grief was a private thing. "He didn't deserve to die like that."

Bridget spoke softly and from close by. "No, he didn't." She pressed a hot cup of coffee and some tissues into his hand. "No one deserves to die like that." Bridget moved away as quietly as she had come. He could hear her moving around by the stove.

He wiped the moisture from his eyes and took a deep, steadying breath. In the glass of the door he could see her reflection.

Somewhere between putting his clothes in the dryer and handing him the coffee, she had located a robe, a thick green thing that covered her from neck to toes. She'd been wearing a blue and white afghan when she had opened the door earlier, and he had gotten a good look at her fantastically shaped legs and what appeared to be a pair of men's boxers. He had liked that view better.

Now she looked like some skinny Christmas tree cracking eggs into a frying pan. He glanced at his own reflection and frowned. He had one hell of a lot of nerve. He was standing in her kitchen wearing nothing but a pair of boxers and a blanket the color of Pepto Bismal. At least now he was warm and dry.

"I hope you like fried eggs." Bridget slid two pieces of toast into the toaster.

He was about to tell her he wasn't hungry when his stomach protested. He needed something in there besides caffeine and anger. He was heading back to the precinct as soon as he left here. "Fried's fine. Can I help with anything?"

Bridget gave him a quick glance and shook her head. "No, thanks. Just sit down. It will be ready in a minute."

He got the impression Bridget was laughing at him. He glanced down and discovered why. Besides looking like some demented flamingo, both his hands were fully occupied. One held his coffee and the other clutched the ends of the blanket together. If he released the blanket, he would end up serving breakfast in his skivvies. Taking the safest route, he sat down and carefully arranged the blanket so everything was covered.

A moment later, Bridget slid a plate filled with eggs and toast in front of him, followed by a glass of orange juice. "Drink it. The vitamin C will help ward off a cold." She joined him with her own breakfast and started to eat.

"Yes, ma'am." Bridget was turning out to be a demanding little thing when she thought she held all the cards. Holding a man dressed only in his underwear virtually hostage was definitely holding all the cards. He would have to explain a few things to her once he got his pants back on. For now, he'd eat. He held the blanket together with one hand and ate with the other.

By the time they were done with breakfast and Bridget had returned from the basement with his dry clothes, he was more than ready for some answers. A quick change in the powder room and he felt more like his old self, more in control. He rejoined Bridget in the kitchen. She had cleared the table and refilled his cup.

He sat back down and studied the dark brew. Bridget had remembered he took his coffee black, no sugar. "It was my turn to buy the coffee."

Bridget crinkled up her forehead, but didn't comment.

"Mark bought it the last time we were out."

Bridget nodded, as if he was making some sense now.

"We stopped at one of those all-night mini markets. It wasn't in the nicest section of town, but we've stopped there before. The coffee is pretty good. Mark stayed in the car while I ran inside."

He looked at his coffee, but couldn't force himself to take a sip. "I don't know when he left the car. I don't even know why. All I know is I paid for the coffee and was leaving the store when the shot rang out. I dropped the coffee, yelled for the owner to call it in, and ran. The alley was two buildings down. Mark was dead before I reached him."

"You didn't see anyone at the entrance to the alley?"

"No one. There was no one there, Bridget."

"Could he have hidden somewhere?"

"Sure. It's possible I ran right by him on my way to the alley. At that moment I was more concerned for Mark than catching the guy." He thought back to the darkened streets, shadowy doorways, and empty buildings. There were a dozen places the shooter could have hidden while Chad ran past. There also had been plenty of time for him to get away before backup arrived.

"What about the rain? Was it raining when you went into the store?"

"It was drizzling." He closed his eyes and thought back to the moment when he pulled into the parking space in front of the mini market. "Mark didn't even have the poncho on when I went into the store. I never connected Mark to your visions until I heard that gunshot. Then I knew." He ran a frustrated hand through his hair. "I knew without even looking in the car Mark wouldn't be there."

"Was it raining when you came out of the store?"

"No, it had stopped." He got up and walked to the patio doors. The rain was still coming down, but it seemed to be letting up some. "Something or someone got him to put on his poncho, leave the car, and walk into that alley."

"How long were you in the store?" Bridget frowned at her own cup.

"Not that long." He matched her frown as the memory of his fixing those two coffees surfaced in his mind. "No, I was there for a couple of minutes. The owner, a real nice guy, had asked me for advice. He knew I was a cop. Hell, anyone in that part of town can pick out a cop at a hundred yards. Anyway, he was concerned about a bunch of kids hanging around the store in the evenings. He has two teenage daughters who help him out by working in the store at night. He wanted to know how to get them to leave without causing any hard feelings. He's scared of repercussions. The neighborhood has been through some rough times recently." He shrugged. "The kids he described seemed pretty harmless to me."

"What advice did you give him?"

"I told him to get uglier daughters." The smile that started to form quickly faded. What the hell did he have to smile about? "I guess I was in there for about five minutes."

"Plenty of time to lure your partner out of the car and into the alley."

"Yeah, plenty of time." He turned and looked at Bridget. She seemed to be thinking about something important. He walked over to the table and sat back down. "What is it?"

"Remember I told you about feeling the killer's thoughts, something about it being the right man, but not the intended victim?"

"Yeah, and that's bothering the hell out of me."

"It should. I've got a feeling we haven't heard the last of him."

"What do you mean *we?*" He didn't like the sound of that. "I told you I don't want you involved in this." He wanted Bridget as far away from this as possible. Maybe she knew something he didn't. "Did you have another vision?"

"No, I had the same one again last night. This time I concentrated on getting a better look at the officer, at your partner." Bridget pushed her cup away. "He's a couple years older than you—I'd say midthirties. His nose probably caused him to be the brunt of more than a few jokes, and he has a dark, thick, bushy mustache."

"*Had,* Bridget, *had.* Mark *had* a mustache and a big nose. He doesn't have anything now. He's dead." He pushed back his chair and stood up.

How was it possible that the simple switching of tense from has to had made a person dead? Gone forever.

He started to pace and studied the tile beneath his feet. Each stride took him over two square tiles. Black, white, black white. He reached the spot in front of the kitchen sink, where a little rug with daisies printed all over it stopped him. For the third time, he turned and glared at Bridget.

"Why didn't you call me? They would have patched you through to me. If you had given me that description, I would have known who it was. I could have prevented Mark from going into that alley."

"I didn't have the vision until after one o'clock, Chad." Bridget clutched her hands together and dropped them into her lap. "I probably was visualizing it while it was happening."

He closed his eyes and clutched at the back of his chair. She was right. It would have been too late. "I shouldn't have yelled at you, Bridget. This is not your fault. You tried to warn me. I just didn't pick up on all the signs."

"It's not your fault." Bridget stood up and walked around to where he was standing. She placed her hand on his arm. "The only one at fault here is the killer. You can't take responsibility for someone else's actions."

"That's true." *But I could have stopped those actions if I would have added two plus two and come up with the right number. Bridget said the officer had brown hair and eyes. I should have known.*

He stared at her delicate fingers resting on the sleeve of his sweatshirt. She was trying to offer him comfort, comfort he didn't need or deserve. Cindy and Mark's two little girls needed the comfort and support. He, on the other hand, was a trained professional. What he needed was justice.

Bridget slowly withdrew her hand and stepped away from him. "There was something different about the vision I had last night."

"What?"

"The gun blast didn't shatter it, like the other times. This time I woke up after"—the hesitation was prolonged—"your partner had fallen."

He picked up on the change. Before it had always been the officer, the cop, and even the policeman. Now she had a name to go with the slain officer.

He had been Chad's partner. His name was Mark. "Anything else?"

"The crack of lightning outside of the house woke me up. When I realized it was pouring out, I got scared and nearly called you. But I figured you'd probably realized it was raining before I had. I turned on The Weather Channel, and they said it was going to rain all night and into the morning. I figured it was safe for one more night."

"It would have been if it hadn't stopped for those five minutes." He watched as Bridget made her way to the patio doors and stared outside. The rain was definitely letting up now. "What else do you remember?"

Bridget hugged herself and continued to look at the rain. "The second chuckle I told you about was clearer. It definitely was laughter, but I still couldn't tell if it came from a male or a low-voiced female. I do know it was moving away. Whoever was laughing was leaving when they were doing it. It faded away, but not with the vision."

"Anything else?"

"Yeah." Bridget reached up and with the tip of one finger followed a lone raindrop as it slowly made its way down the pane of glass. "Remember those thoughts I keep feeling?"

"Right man, but not the intended victim?"

"That's one of them."

"What's the other one?" He braced himself for the blow to come. Bridget wouldn't look at him. It had to be bad.

"When the laughter was fading and the killer leaving, I got one more of his thoughts."

"Which was?"

Bridget hesitated for so long, he could tell by the stiffness in her posture she knew he wasn't going to like what she had to say.

"It was easier than he'd thought it would be." Bridget faced him and hugged herself tighter. "I'm sorry, Chad. I'm not sure if he was referring to luring your partner into the alley and getting him alone, or if he meant the actual killing."

"Christ, what kind of killer are we dealing with?" The acid in the pit of his stomach churned. He felt physically ill. Killing Mark had been easier than the killer had thought.

"One who will strike again, I'm afraid." Bridget cringed under his glare. "Remember, Chad, he didn't get his intended victim."

"So who's his intended victim? Another man? Another officer? Someone connected to Mark or his family?" The list could be endless. There was no way of knowing without another variable.

"You." Bridget's voice was barely above a whisper. "The intended victim could be you, Chad."

"Me? Why me?"

"Why not you?"

"Because it doesn't make any sense. They could have lured me into that alley or any other alley and shot me instead. Mark was a good cop. He wasn't easily fooled. Why kill him if I was the intended victim?"

"Why kill him at all, Chad? It doesn't make sense. It wasn't as if he was working a case and cornered a desperate criminal in that alley. The criminal cornered an unsuspecting Mark and then shot him in cold blood."

"So you're telling me someone planned to kill Mark?"

"Yes, it was planned, but I won't swear Mark was in the plans."

"What are you talking about?" He couldn't believe he was standing here arguing theories with Bridget. She might have seen a vision, but she knew squat about how a criminal mind worked.

"It's one of two ways, Chad. The killer might have been near that mini market and saw you and Mark, recognized you as cops, and decided on the spur of the moment to take one of you out. The killer would have had no idea a pair of cops would be pulling up for some coffee. It would have been a case of Mark's being in the wrong place at the wrong time."

He couldn't argue with the logic of that. "What's the other way, Sherlock?"

Bridget didn't rise to his barb. "The killer knew who he wanted to kill and had been following you and Mark. When you disappeared into the store, it was his opportunity. At that time of the morning and with the rain, the streets were probably deserted. Simple enough to find a dead-end alley to trap someone, once he got him into it."

"So you're saying the killer planned on killing Mark all along?" Try as he might, he couldn't think of one thing Mark might have done to warrant being killed like that. As far as he knew, Mark had never given anyone a raw deal. In fact, the total opposite

could be said. In the five years they had been together they never acted out the good-cop, bad-cop
routine. They *were* the good cop, bad cop.

"I didn't say that, Chad. Maybe he would have
killed you if Mark had gone in for coffee." A shudder
wracked her body. "Maybe Mark's being a cop had
nothing to do with it. Maybe he was killed because
he was a Catholic or had dark hair or used to date
the killer's sister." Bridget turned away from him and
bent to pick up the black cat that had just strolled
into the room.

The cat must have picked up on Bridget's aggra-
vation, because it rubbed its head against her chest
and glared daggers at him. He shifted uneasily under
that hostile golden stare. If he had been a mouse,
his head wouldn't still be attached to his body. He
nodded to the cat curled against her chest. "Who's
your buddy there?"

"Shamrock. She's the boss around here." Bridget's
fingers scratched and petted the cat. "I bet you're
hungry, Shammy. It's way past your breakfast time."
Bridget put the cat down and pulled a can of cat
food from a cabinet.

Bridget looked so damned domestic with her no-
frills bathrobe, sleep-tossed hair, and a cat rubbing
its way between and around her bare feet. A man
could do worse than waking up to the sight of her
every morning for the rest of his life. He needed to
put another five years' distance between them.

He glanced at his watch. "Speaking of time, I have
to leave." He bent and pulled on his wet sneakers.

"If you remember anything else from the visions, call me either at home or at work."

Arguing theories with Bridget wasn't getting him anywhere. He needed to get back to the precinct to see what else they might have discovered. He reached for his jacket.

Bridget walked him to the front door. "If I think of anything, I'll call." She touched his arm. "Chad, do me a favor."

"What?" Why was she making this so damned difficult? All he wanted to do was leave. Her soft green eyes had gone softer and her mouth seemed to tremble before his very eyes.

"Be careful out there."

Out there was a picnic compared to what was in here. There was more danger in this very house than in the entire city of Philadelphia. Out on the street he might lose his life, but with Bridget he would lose his heart. He had known that five years ago and had the strength to walk away. He could only pray to have the same strength now. "I will."

He reached out and tenderly caressed her cheek with the palm of his hand.

Her eyes seemed to beg him for something he couldn't give.

"You take care, Bridget." With one last look he turned and walked away.

He had a killer to catch and a woman to forget.

FOUR

Chad sat in the loneliness of his living room and closed his eyes. The silence washed over him. Sometimes living alone had its drawbacks, and tonight was one of them.

Why hadn't he noticed the oppressive silence before? It felt as if the walls were closing in on him. He could be standing in the middle of the room screaming his soul to shreds, and no one would hear. No one would care.

The endless silence and lack of another's presence was getting on his nerves. Then again, everything had been getting on his nerves lately.

Five days ago he had stood in the pouring rain beside a black shining casket and watched as it was lowered into the ground. Mark was gone. Since then, he had put in fourteen-hour days, asked more than a thousand questions of a hundred different strangers, and pounded more pavements than he cared to think about. He was not one step closer to discovering who had killed his partner or even why.

The general consensus on the street was Mark had died because he was a cop. Anyone who hadn't known he was a cop when he had gotten out of the car had learned it the moment he had pulled on the standard police-issue poncho.

The killer had known he was a cop before pulling that trigger, but it didn't mean Mark was shot because he was a cop. Maybe it didn't matter one way or the other.

Every officer on the force had pulled in favors, pressed their sources for information, and had come up with the same answers Chad had. Nothing. The word on the streets was there was no word, and that made everybody nervous.

Something of this magnitude didn't get swept under a carpet. Someone had to know something, someone had to brag and boast, but no one was talking. Killing a cop was big news in any city, and people always talked. There would be no way of containing the word once it hit the streets.

The police commissioner was demanding answers. The media kept speculating about what the department's official "no comment" and "we're following up on some leads" meant. A task force had been assigned the case, and he knew he was being investigated. Mark had been his partner and he had been at the scene.

He knew the procedure and wasn't worried about having the task force dig up any dirt. They wouldn't find any. He was more concerned with the lack of any leads, solid or otherwise. Fellow officers were getting edgy, looking over their shoulders, and second-guessing every situation. No one liked having a cop killer on the streets.

Tonight was his first night home before the evening news in over a week. He should be enjoying the solitude instead of cursing it. Maybe he should follow Bridget's example and get a cat. A cat would keep him company and give him someone—or was it something?—to talk to.

He pictured the arrogant look her cat had given him and chuckled. That cat definitely had an attitude problem. Then again, he couldn't blame the poor creature. Bridget had named her after a weed.

Shamrock. What kind of name was that for a cat, anyway, especially a female cat? Had she been hoping to toughen it up into an attack cat?

He could just picture it now. Bridget standing there alone and unprotected, shouting, "Attack, Shammy, attack!" as burglars busted down her front door.

A shudder went through him as he stood up and paced to the sliding glass door. Bridget needed a dog, a big, vicious, trained dog named Killer or Terminator, a dog criminals wouldn't fail to notice or heed. She also needed an alarm system. A woman living alone couldn't be too careful. Everywhere you looked, bad things happened to good people. He didn't want anything bad to happen to Bridget. She had been through enough.

He hadn't seen her since he'd left her house the morning after his partner had died. Just because he hadn't seen her didn't mean she hadn't been on his mind. The woman had been playing complete and utter havoc with his mind all week long.

More than once he'd had to stop himself from calling her just to make sure she was all right. Once when he found himself in the northeast section of the city, he'd even driven by her flower shop. The Garden of Eden was an end store in a very busy strip mall. There had been quite a few cars parked outside of it, including Bridget's. The temptation to stop in to check on her had been great, but he had resisted.

Tonight he couldn't resist knowing if she'd had any more dreams or if she was finally sleeping better. She had looked like hell the last two times he'd seen her. He could pick up the phone and call, but that wouldn't stop the apartment from closing in on him. He needed to get out and see for himself that she was doing okay.

Half an hour later, he pulled up in front of her house, turned his car off, and got out. By the number of lights gleaming through her windows and her car in the driveway, he'd have to say she was home.

Last week when he was here, he hadn't noticed her house or the neighborhood. He vaguely remembered a porch, but that was about it for the exterior. Tonight he took his time and glanced up and down the tree-lined street. Everything was quiet, and the houses all looked neat and well kept.

Bridget's was no exception. He guessed it had been built in the forties and was called an Arts and Crafts bungalow. The street was lined with the same type of houses. There was a short front yard, most of it filled with flower gardens overflowing with plants and an enormous oak tree in magnificent fall color. One side yard was nonexistent, while the other was only wide enough for some bushes and the driveway that went along the side of the house to the back-yard. He assumed there was a garage in the back, but he hadn't noticed it the other day. He had noticed some nice sized trees and a patio back there, but that was about all.

The well-lit porch ran the entire width of the cream-colored house. Dark green trim and rockers with thick flowery cushions added a homey feel. So did the dozen potted chrysanthemums scattered about the porch and the two steps leading to it. One of those twig-type wreaths with a colorful bow hung from the front door. The whole house looked lived in and loved.

He made his way up onto the porch, admiring the different flowers as he went. For late September, he was impressed with everything that was still in bloom. He couldn't imagine what Bridget's yard looked like in the middle of summer or even spring.

His finger went to the doorbell before he remembered it didn't work. Two wires wrapped in electrical tape were sticking out of the hole. He knocked on the door and waited.

A moment later he heard Bridget before she even opened the door. "Oh, you're early tonight."

He raised an eyebrow and met her confused expression as she opened the door. "I didn't realize you were expecting me at all." Wasn't that pushing clairvoyance too far?

"I wasn't." Bridget blushed at her abrupt reply. "I mean, I was expecting Shane." Bridget glanced up and down the street, shrugged her shoulders, and opened the door wider. "Come on in, Chad."

"Who's Shane?" So much for his theory that she didn't have a boyfriend hanging around. A woman didn't look like Bridget and stay unattached for long.

A noisy, mufflerless car pulling up in front of her house prevented her from answering and closing the door. A kid with blue spiked hair and a dozen earrings in various body parts, sprinted his way to the door, carrying a pizza box. "Hey, Ms. Mackenzie, just the way you like it—hot with extra cheese."

The boy gave Chad an appraising look and then puffed out his underdeveloped chest. His voice deepened as he asked, "Is this guy bothering you, Ms. Mac?"

Chad had to give the boy credit for having guts. Not only did he have fifty pounds and roughly twelve years over the kid, but there was a good eight-inch difference in height if you didn't count the spikes. He liked the way the kid stood his ground and was willing to protect Bridget.

"No, Shane, he's not bothering me. He's a friend. Chad, meet Shane, a local neighborhood kid and the reigning king of pizza delivery. Shane, meet Chad, a friend."

Shane grinned. Not only were his bottom lip and tongue pierced, but he still had an orthodontic retainer in his mouth. "Hot date, Ms. Mac?" He handed Bridget the pizza.

"No, Shane, just friends." Bridget handed Shane the money she had been clutching when she answered Chad's knock. "Keep the change. Put it to a new muffler before you get a ticket."

Shane jammed the bill into his pocket. "Thanks,

Ms. Mac, but no can do. There's a new Bleached Blond Bimbos enhanced CD that's top of the line rad." Shane gave Chad one last glance, bobbed his head, and said "Cool," before disappearing back into his car and backfiring his way down the street.

Chad looked at Bridget and raised one brow. "Did you get any of that?"

"Music." Bridget shifted the hot pizza to her other hand and shut the door. "I heard a CD in there, so it must be music." She carefully maneuvered her way around ladders and drop cloths and headed for the kitchen. "I hope you like sausage and extra cheese on your pizza."

"Is that an invitation?" The smell of the pizza had been making his mouth water. He had skipped lunch to question the teenage boys who hung out at the mini market to check out the owner's daughters. They swore they knew nothing, and he had to believe them. Another brick wall. He hadn't even realized he was hungry until the aroma of the pizza hit him. Skipped meals had been the norm for him this past week.

"Sure. You don't think I'm going to eat all this do you?" Bridget opened the box and pulled two plates from the cabinet. "There's soda and beer in the refrigerator. Help yourself, but grab me a beer, please."

Bridget was drinking a beer with her pizza! If ever there was a woman after his own heart, she had to be it. Pizza and beer. The woman knew how to live right.

He opened the refrigerator and pulled out two

beers. An entire shelf was devoted to beer, soda, and bottled water. "You planning a party?" It would take Bridget a month of Mexican dinners to drink all of that.

"No, two of my brothers were here for the weekend and that's what's left." Bridget grabbed two bags of chips from a cabinet and added them to the table. "When they're away from the wives and kids, they turn back into a bunch of frat boys. They eat cold pizza and Chinese food for breakfast, continuous tacos and nachos from lunch till dinner, and then they call to have something totally unhealthy delivered."

"Sounds like an antacid commercial." He sat down, twisted the caps off the beers, and handed her one. "They visit often?" Being an only child and then orphaned at an early age left a lot of holes in his concept of family life. Bridget's brothers didn't sound like the Hallmark family he had always pictured.

"They weren't visiting, really. They were working." Bridget handed him a plate with a slice of pizza on it. "I have four older brothers, all married, and there's nine—no, make that ten—kids between them so far." Bridget bit into a slice and chewed. "I was just informed number eleven will be arriving sometime around Easter."

He raised his beer and saluted her. "Sounds like a productive family." Eleven nieces and nephews. He couldn't imagine it. Christmas alone would push his lone credit card over the max.

Bridget smiled. "Anyway, since my brothers and their wives like to take some time and get away alone without the kids, we all take turns babysitting. Mom and Dad can't handle it all, so we share the joy. A few days here and there throughout the year and everyone is happy."

"And nine months later you get another niece or nephew, right?"

This time Bridget's smile turned into a full-blown grin. "Usually."

Bridget's smile went straight to his head. Lord, she was breathtaking when she did that. He glanced down at his plate and concentrated on their conversation. "That doesn't seem fair. They babysit each other's kids and get a babysitter in return. What do you get out of it?"

"Hard physical and manual work." Bridget nodded toward the living room. "Didn't you notice the difference? Connor and Brian worked their butts off last weekend to get it ready for me to paint."

"I noticed it was all white now, instead of sheet rock gray and spackle. The rest of the room looked the same." Drop cloths, ladders, and paint cans were scattered throughout, just like the other day.

"The drop cloths are covering the newly done floor. They finished the ceiling for me and wired in the lights by Saturday afternoon. By Saturday night, the walls were sanded and primed and the trim was back up. By Sunday, they had the entire oak floor sanded down to bare wood. They even stained it for me before they left. I wouldn't be able to do a third of the things that have been done around here. Contractors are too expensive. Besides, Sean and Brian own their own construction company and I get everything at cost."

"Not a bad deal, I guess." He finished off his first slice and reached for the second. "Does your family still live out in . . . what was it, Reading?" He remembered her family hadn't lived in Philly and that one of her brothers owned a pub.

"Either in the city or close by. I'm the only one who doesn't. It caused quite a stir when I didn't move home after I graduated."

"Why didn't you?" He had kept tabs on her after she was released from the hospital. He thought for sure she would have gone home then, but she hadn't. Bridget had surprised him and then earned his respect when she went directly back to the same campus and completed her degree on time. The woman had guts, but then she had once confided in him that she was known as the stubborn one in the family. He could see why.

"I like the city." Bridget shrugged and tried to ignore Chad's look of disbelief. She knew what he was thinking. How could she like this city after what had happened to her here? She didn't blame the city for what had happened. She blamed a sick individual, and it was a sad fact that sick individuals lived just about anywhere. "I like my independence. Being the baby of a family and having four overprotective older brothers has its drawbacks." She playfully shuddered at some of the memories.

"Like what?"

Chad seemed curious, and for some unexplained reason that pleased her. She had been pleasantly surprised and totally unprepared when she'd opened the door earlier and found him standing there instead of Shane.

Tonight she had planned on painting the living room and had dressed accordingly in a pair of paint-smeared jeans and a T-shirt one of her brothers had left behind. Her hair was yanked back into a ponytail and thick sweat socks covered her feet. She felt about as attractive as a slug.

What did it matter how she felt? Chad hadn't come to see her because he was interested in her as a woman. So far he hadn't brought up the visions or anything regarding his partner's death, but that didn't mean this wasn't a professional visit.

Chad wanted to know about her life with her brothers. She gave him a personal answer, just to see what he would do. "I wasn't allowed to date any of their friends."

"Why not?"

"Because they all swore they knew what their friends were capable of, and I wasn't allowed anywhere near them. With four older brothers, that severely limited my dating options. When I did meet someone in school, it was like the Spanish Inquisition—without the executions, of course. When I came here for school, I was given my first taste of freedom, and I liked it."

Her freshman year at college had been a total disaster when it came to her personal life. She purposely dated every boy her brothers would have punched in the nose for so much as talking to her. Years and maturity later, she could admit her brothers had been mostly right. By her second year, she had calmed down. By the third, she had a steady boyfriend. By her senior year, she was once again alone, but hadn't minded. Her schoolwork had taken priority in her life.

"If I lived anywhere near my family, they'd be dropping over at all hours of the day and night just to check up on me. I love them all dearly, and I know they only want what's good for me, but I can't live like that. No one asked for my approval before any of my brothers asked a girl out on a date. It was assumed they all knew what they were doing, while I, the lone female, hadn't a clue." She gave him a small shrug and prayed she hadn't bored him to tears. "Didn't you have a sister or two to boss around and make miserable?"

"No sisters or brothers. I was an only child." Chad finished off the crust of his second slice. "I never knew my father, and my mother died when I was eight."

"Oh, God, Chad. I'm sorry." Here she had been going on about how terrible it was having an over-protective family. "Who raised you, a grandmother?"

"No, I didn't have one of those either that I knew of. I was raised through the system, and no matter what anyone says, the system works. I turned out okay." Chad finished off his beer. "Were you going to paint tonight?"

The change in subject was abrupt and to the point. Chad didn't want to talk about his past. She couldn't blame him. He claimed he had turned out okay, and on the outside he had. He was an upstanding member of the community and a dedicated police officer. But what about on the inside, where it counted the most? Why didn't he have a family of his own?

She glanced down at the faded, oversized T-shirt advertising Connor's pub, The Blarney Stone, that she was wearing, and smiled. "I don't usually go around advertising my brother's pub." The three-inch tear near the hem added to the ensemble's allure.

"Need any help?"

"You want to help me paint?" Now he was really confusing her. No one ever offered to help someone else paint. It wasn't a job too many people enjoyed.

"Sure. This is the second time you've fed me. It's the least I could do."

"You haven't painted much, have you?" Two meals didn't constitute hours of tedious manual labor.

"Not much, but I'm willing."

Chad looked so sincere she didn't have the heart to tell him no.

"Okay. I can't do much about your pants, but I'm sure I've got another one of my brothers' old T-shirts upstairs." She got up, rinsed out the empty bottles, and deposited them in the recycling bin on the back patio. Shamrock came strolling in when she opened the patio doors. "Well, hello. Are we done exploring for the night?"

Shamrock purred and walked in and out between her legs.

"Aren't you afraid she'll run away?" Chad put the plates in the dishwasher as he watched the cat greet Bridget.

"Shammy, run away?" Bridget chuckled and picked up the spoiled cat. "She has it too good here to go looking elsewhere." She put the cat down and placed two treats by Shammy's water bowl. "The backyard is fenced in and she loves exploring all the flower gardens, but she never stays out for more than an hour or two."

Shamrock swallowed both tiny fish-shaped treats without chewing and then stared at Chad.

"I don't think she likes me." Chad stared back at the cat.

She almost giggled. Chad had sounded so dejected by the idea of her cat's not liking him. "She's just checking you out and trying to decide if you're a threat to her domain."

"Tell her I'm harmless." Chad squatted and held out a hand. "Come here, girl."

Shamrock looked at the offending hand, lifted her nose into the air, and strolled out of the room with more dignity than a queen.

Chad stood back up. "See, I told you."

She couldn't help it. She giggled. "She's not a dog, Chad. Cats don't usually come to people on command. They're independent and arrogant creatures. Shamrock basically allows me to share this home with her."

"I only have one word for you. Fish." Chad shut the dishwasher's door. "Goldfish."

She bit her lower lip to keep from giggling again. "Isn't that two words?" She headed out of the kitchen to get him a different shirt. "The stereo's in there." She nodded to what eventually would be the dining room, but for now held her living room furniture. "Put on whatever you like. Music helps the work go faster."

Five minutes later, Chad came out of the powder room wearing one of Sean's old shirts. Bridget felt her mouth go dry and she quickly dropped her gaze back to the paint can in her hand. That shirt had never looked like that on Sean. How in the world was she going to get through the next several hours with him dressed in tight jeans and a shirt that clung to him like skin? She'd hoped her brother's shirt would give him a brotherly feel, but what she felt toward Chad definitely wasn't brotherly.

"Pink! You're painting the room pink?" Chad stopped in the middle of the room and stared at the paint tray as if it were a live cobra.

"It's not pink." She used the brush and wiped off the lip of the can so the paint didn't drip. She liked this color and refused to buckle under male opinion. Her brothers had given her a hard time about her choice of color, too, until she had pointed out that Brian's master bedroom was lilac and Connor had just painted his daffodil yellow. They had kept their opinions to themselves after that, but Chad was a different matter. Chad was Mr. Beige. He had no sense of color. In fact, he had no color at all. Beige and brown weren't colors, in her book.

"What color is it if it isn't pink?"

"It's Iced Raspberry." She handed him the roller. "You roll and I'll do the hand cutting in." She climbed a ladder and carefully started to paint the wall's edge where it met the ceiling. "You have rolled on paint before, right?"

"A couple of times." Chad rolled the roller around in the tray of paint until it was evenly covered. "I'll wait until you get a good start on the wall before I begin."

"The cutting in takes longer than the rolling on, I'm afraid."

"That's okay." Chad put the roller down and walked over to a window to glance outside. "What made you buy a house that needed so much work?"

"Besides being affordable and allowing me the opportunity to do things my way?" She concentrated on the painting.

"Besides that."

"I hated apartment living. I needed gardens and trees around me. The neighborhood is great and there's a sense of community among us." She moved the ladder and continued painting. "Why do you live in an apartment?"

"It's simple and there's no hassle. Pay the rent and call the super if there's a problem." Chad leaned against the windowsill and watched her. "I wouldn't know how to plant a flower if it came with directions."

"They do."

"Do what?"

"Come with directions. Most plants you buy come with a plastic little label that tells you how and where to plant." She reached the end of the wall, climbed down, and started to paint where the wall met the baseboard. It was easier going, because she had spent last night taping around everything. "Do you like flowers, Chad?"

"Well, they look pretty and smell good."

"So do supermodels."

Chad grinned. "I like those."

She shook her head and smiled. "So does every male above the age of twelve." She couldn't talk to Chad about his past. Scratch the subject of houses or flowers, which basically was her whole life. That only left one other topic she knew enough about for a decent conversation—football. She hadn't lived with four brothers for nothing. She could probably hold her own on the subject of hockey too, but she preferred Philadelphia's football team. "So, Chad, what do you think the Eagles' chances are this year?" She felt Chad's gaze on her, but she refused to look up. She crawled along the baseboard and painted.

"Chances for what? Making the playoffs?" When she reached the end of the wall he picked up the roller and started to paint.

"What other chances are there?"

Over the next two and a half hours, they painted all four walls and the short hallway. The only area left to paint was the stairwell wall, the dread of any homeowner with a second floor.

Bridget handed Chad a bottle of water. "So, Leonardo, any ideas?" She had been teasing him about his natural painting ability since she'd realized what a great job he had been doing. She had originally resigned herself to having to do two coats when she learned of his limited experience with a roller.

After the first wall was done, her hopes had risen. One coat was going to do it.

She watched entranced as Chad drank over half the bottle at once. He just tilted back his head and drank. Her gaze went to his throat and was riveted by the play of muscles and the bobbing of his Adam's apple. A light sheen of moisture coated his skin and the bristly shadow of his beard had made an appearance. Chad was one hundred percent pure male and she was alone with him in her house.

Instead of being terrified of him, she was excited. Maybe excited was too strong a word, but she definitely felt alive for the first time in years. She felt like a woman who was in the company of a very desirable man.

Chad lowered the water bottle and stared back at her. She couldn't read the emotion that had leaped into his eyes. It was there one moment and gone the next. She would be fooling herself if she thought it was an answering desire. No man could possibly desire her looking like this. She was the one to break eye contact.

"I guess we could only paint up eight feet or so." The wall went up the entire height of the second floor. It was sixteen or seventeen feet high in places, with nothing but stairs below. There was nowhere to safely put a ladder. She would just have to wait until one of her brothers needed a baby-sitter.

"That would look like hell, Bridget. You'd be able to see where you stopped painting from the living room. You need to paint the entire thing." Chad walked up the steps, and then back down. He studied it from every angle.

"Have any ideas?"

"Any of your brothers leave any lumber around here? I'm talking ten-, twelve-foot planks."

"In the basement there's some. Why?"

"Show me." Chad had gotten that excited manly gleam in his eyes that she recognized from her brothers. She knew it would be useless to argue, so she led the way to the basement corner where her brothers had stored stuff for future use.

Chad took two seconds to find what he needed. "Help me bring it upstairs."

Fifteen minutes later, she regretted helping him haul the heavy board up the basement stairs. "Are you crazy, Chad? That won't hold your weight." The board was now suspended from the ladder to the top stair. It was a ten-inch-wide tightrope without a net. It looked like one of her brothers' hare-brained ideas.

"Sure it will." Chad stepped onto the board. It bowed and bounced slightly with his weight. "See? Now hand me the roller."

One hour and three gray hairs later, the stairwell was done, the plank put back in the basement, and everything was put away for the night. Chad was washing the last of the paint from his hands at the kitchen sink.

"How about some coffee?" They had taken a break halfway through the job to polish off the rest of the pizza. Chad looked like a man with the same appetite as her brothers, the bottomless pits, as her mother had once jokingly referred to her sons. Her own food bill when they came to visit was testimony to that.

"No, thanks, Bridget. It's getting late and I have to be at the station by seven." Chad dried his hands and put on his jacket. He had changed shirts only moments before.

She walked him to the front door. "Thanks for helping. It turned a two-night job into a one-night job." She still didn't know what to make of his visit. He hadn't once mentioned the visions or his partner's death. The newspaper had given Mark Monterey's murder front page space for three days in a row. She had cried when they ran a full-color photo of the graveside service. A young woman with two little girls clinging to her hands stood next to the flower-draped casket. Now it was usually given a paragraph or two buried somewhere in the paper, just to let everyone know it was still unsolved.

"Thanks for dinner." Chad opened the door, but didn't step out onto the porch. He stood there and stared at her face for a long time. With a tender touch, he traced a line down her cheek. "You have a streak of pink paint on your cheek."

"Iced Raspberry." She sighed as the warmth of his finger caressed her cheek, and she felt lightheaded. It was either a reaction to his touch or the paint fumes. She knew where she would bet her money.

Chad slowly smiled, and that heated look returned to his eyes she had once classed as ordinary brown. She now knew better. They were deep chocolate with flecks of gold. "Thank you, Bridget." His voice sounded rough and uneven.

"For what?"

"For giving me an enjoyable evening. For talking about ordinary stuff and taking my mind off the case for a couple of hours." Chad brushed back a lock of hair that had escaped the ponytail. Her mouth went dry with anticipation. Chad was going to kiss her—she could see it in his eyes. The gold flecks were sparking. "For just being Bridget Erin Mackenzie, a very desirable, interesting, and colorful woman."

Chad pressed his warm lips against her forehead for a moment, and then he was gone.

She stared after him in stunned silence.

Chad was halfway down the walk when he turned and said, "Do me a favor."

"What?" She cringed at the breathless, bewildered quality of her voice.

"Get yourself a dog." Chad turned, got into his car, and drove away.

She stood there on her porch and watched as the taillights disappeared down the road. A dog? Her knees felt like they were melting through the wooden slats of her porch, and he wanted her to buy a dog. She went back into the house and closed the door.

She glanced at the freshly painted walls of the living room and knew where Chad had come up with "colorful" in his description of her. "Interesting" was probably a nice, proper way of referring to her clairvoyant dreams. It was "desirable" she was having trouble with. If she was all that desirable, why hadn't he kissed her? That brotherly buzz across the forehead didn't count as a kiss in her book. Her three-year-old nephew kissed with more passion.

Then again, her three-year-old nephew hadn't been around five years ago to see her body used and beaten. Her trembling hand rose to the mark encircling her throat, a reminder of the past she could never forget. Neither could Chad.

Sighing heavily, she locked the door and slid on the chain. Chad had lied. He hadn't found her desirable and he never would.

FIVE

Late Sunday night, Bridget paced the small confines of her bedroom. It was happening again! It couldn't be happening again, but it was. Why? What had she ever done to warrant this?

For a blessed week and a half, there'd been nothing but silence and her own sweet dreams, and now this. She hadn't seen or heard from Chad since Wednesday night, when he'd given her his bewildering parting shot about buying a dog.

She had been tempted on more than one occasion to call him and see what that meant, but she hadn't. Chad obviously didn't want to see her again, or he would have called or stopped by over the weekend. He'd done neither, and she had been home most of the time putting the finishing touches to the living room.

Now she had to call him—and tell him what? She wasn't sure. She had to tell someone, and Chad was the obvious choice. Last night the vision had been weak and distorted. When she had awakened in the middle of the night, she had been unsure if it had been a vision or a nightmare. She had prayed for a nightmare. Now she knew it hadn't been. The visions were back.

She pulled on her robe and offered Shamrock, who was standing and stretching on her bed, an apology. "Sorry for disturbing your beauty sleep, Shammy." Shamrock had almost ended up on the floor when Bridget had jerked out of the vision earlier.

The cat arched her back and stretched her front paws out farther before hopping off the bed and following Bridget from the room.

The dim light at the top of the stairs allowed her to descend them and once again admire the room below. The living room had turned out extremely well and had been worth all the hard work and money. She still needed a few assorted pieces of furniture to complete it, but if she stayed on her budget, all would be done by Christmas—just in time for her brothers and their wives to take a few ski weekends in the Poconos and for her to earn some free manual labor. She loved watching her nieces and nephews, as long as they came in small, manageable numbers. The dining room was next on her list.

In the kitchen, she flipped on the light and grabbed the telephone book to look up Chad's number. She had no idea if he was home or on duty, but she had to try. Shamrock curled around her feet and purred.

"No, Shammy, no more treats tonight. You might think it's your fur fluffing out, but let me tell you, it isn't." Shamrock sauntered out of the room with her tail in the air as Bridget dialed Chad's number. On the second ring he picked up.

"Yeah?" His voice was low and rough with sleep.

Visions of rumpled sheets and satisfied smiles played across her mind. Her voice was nearly as husky as his. "Chad, it's me, Bridget. I'm sorry for waking you."

"God, not another one." The weariness and vulnerability in his voice tugged at her heart.

How could she keep doing this to him? She didn't have a choice in the matter, but he deserved one. "Tell me to hang up and I will."

Chad hesitated long enough for her to know he was considering it, and considering it hard. With a weary sigh, he said, "Tell me about it."

"It's not clear at all, Chad. I had the first vision last night and I couldn't tell if it was real or if it was a nightmare."

"Why didn't you call me then?" The sleep had disappeared from his voice and with it the visions of rumpled sheets. Chad was all business now.

"I wasn't sure. I didn't want to drag you into it until I was sure."

"Now you're sure?" There was a hint of hope in his voice, as if he wanted her not to be sure.

"Now I'm sure." She waited for him to make another comment. He didn't. "It's night . . ."

"Why is it always night?"

"I don't know, Chad. Maybe because most criminals like to do their work under cover of darkness. Do you want me to continue, or do you want to question the position of the moon, too?"

"You saw the moon?" Chad's voice raised in excitement. "That could help us determine when . . ."

"No, I didn't see the moon. I'm sorry. I was just being smart." She closed her eyes and leaned her head against a kitchen cabinet. God, could she feel any worse? She'd been the one to wake him out of a sound sleep, not the other way around. What gave her the right to get smart with him?

"It's getting to you, isn't it?"

Chad's voice held so much understanding that she wanted to cry. Tears wouldn't make it go away, and they wouldn't help. Tears were utterly useless, and she refused to give in to them tonight.

Grandmom Rosalie's words played across her mind. *The Good Lord only gives you what you can handle.* Not for the first time she wondered why her grandmother would lie to her. "Yes, it's getting to me."

The silence on the other end lengthened until she nearly let the tears win.

"Can you tell me what happened?" Chad's voice held no emotion at all. He was Detective Chad Barnett questioning a witness, a witness to a crime that hadn't even been committed yet. It made her feel somewhat better. If he had been all sympathetic and understanding, she probably wouldn't be able to get through this without a big emotional scene. It was one of the qualities that made Chad such a good cop. He knew how to handle a witness, even over the phone.

"It's night. There's a streetlight in the distance, but not where the two men are."

"Two?"

"Two. They're walking. I see their backs and they appear to be kidding each other. You know, joking and joshing around about something." She kept her eyes closed and concentrated. "There are cars parked around them, like they're in a parking lot. Buildings are up ahead, but I can't see them, really. I just know they're there. A car comes speeding toward them. They don't see it or hear it until it's a few yards behind them, and then it's too late. No headlights are on. The car never slowed down, Chad. It hit them both. They went flying into the air just as I woke up."

"Can you describe the car?"

"Dark. Four doors, I think, and a sedan." She moved away from the cabinet. "I'm not very good at makes of cars, Chad. They all look the same to me, unless it something obvious like a Volkswagen Beetle or a minivan."

"That's okay. Tell me about the taillights. Were they square, long, or round? What about a license plate? Was it a Pennsylvania one? Did you see any numbers or letters? Bumper stickers?"

"No, no, and no. I just saw the men thrown into the air like rag dolls. I didn't notice anything about the car."

"Okay, tell me what you can about the men?"

How could Chad sound so unemotional, so in control when the world was falling apart around them and hell was sucking them in?

Her hand tightened on the receiver. "They're African-Americans. Short hair. I can't judge the height, but I'll guess average. There's not much difference in their heights. They aren't overweight. They appear to be in good physical shape, anywhere from young adult to middle-aged. I couldn't see their faces when they both turned around and spotted the car. It was too dark and it happened too quickly. They didn't even have time to get out of the way."

"What about clothes?"

"One was wearing a Flyers jacket. I recognized the bright orange and black logo. The other had on some type of dark jacket with a hood. It looked like one of those hooded sweatshirts. Dark pants, but I couldn't tell you if they were jeans or not." She concentrated harder. "A duffel bag. There was a duffel bag in there somewhere. I saw it go flying."

"Can you describe the bag?"

"Dark." She glanced at the bright yellow kitchen wall and wondered whatever possessed her to paint it that color. She didn't deserve to live in a cheerful, bright home. She should be cooking in a damp, musty basement with a bubbling black cauldron. *Bubble, bubble, toil and trouble!* Heck, she already had the black cat. All she needed were some bats and a black pointy hat.

"Bridget?" Chad had to say her name twice to get her attention. "Are you all right?"

"Just peachy." She cringed. She really had to work on the vocabulary. Predictors of doom and gloom didn't say "peachy."

"You sound funny. Are you sure you're all right?"

The concern in Chad's voice pulled her back to their conversation. She could worry about her retreat from sanity later. Right now she needed to give Chad every bit of information she could remember. "Sorry, just tired."

"Do you see a connection between this hit-and-run and Mark's death?"

"No, but it's a logical question. I've already given it some thought. I can't see any connection."

"Could the two men be cops?"

"They could be just about anything, but I can't see any signs of their being cops. No uniforms, no guns, and no badges. I didn't get any gut feelings one way or another."

"What about their location? Any ideas where it might be?"

"It's about as generic as the alley. I'll say in the city somewhere, but that's about as close as I can guess. No huge office buildings or museums, though."

"What about the driver of the car? Any feelings? Could there have been more than one person in the car?"

"I couldn't tell how many people were in the car. The driver could have been male or female, and I didn't pick up any feelings one way or the other."

"Could it be the same person who killed Mark?"

She knew what Chad wanted. He wanted a common denominator. He wanted a connection between the two crimes. There were no leads in Mark's murder, and this would give him something to go on. How he would explain it down at the precinct was another matter. He would be working a lead that hadn't even happened yet. She couldn't give him what he wanted. "I'm sorry, Chad. I don't know."

A heavy sigh reached her ear. "Stop apologizing to me every three minutes, Bridget. It's not your fault you don't know every answer. If you did, I could go out and just arrest the guy. Hell, the city would put you on its payroll and cut crime in half with one good night's sleep."

She could see it now. She'd head up the psychic dream squad and Chad would go out and arrest criminals for just thinking up a crime. Heck, maybe he'd arrest them before they even thought up the offense.

"Chad, do you think I have the vision once the killer has the idea and I'm actually seeing the planning stage? Or do you think I'm seeing it before the killer even thinks up his next act of violence?"

"Hell if I know. Does it make a difference?"

"I guess not." *But did it? Would it be easier to change the future if the act hadn't even been planned yet?*

"Do you remember anything else?" Chad yawned and tried to muffle it. She heard it anyway.

"No, that's it." She wrapped the cord around one of her fingers. "If I think of anything else or learn anything more, I'll give you a call."

Chad needed his sleep. Wednesday night she had seen the circles under his eyes and the edge of fatigue pulling at him. She shouldn't have called. How was he to stop a crime that hadn't even happened yet, especially when she couldn't even tell him who, what, where, or when?

"If I'm not home and it's important, call the precinct."

"Sure. Good night, Chad."

"One last question before you go, Bridget."

"What?"

"Do the men live? Do you think they survived the hit-and- run?"

She didn't want to think about that part, the sickening sound of the impact, the heavy thuds as bone and muscle met steel and speed. That was the part she dreaded the most about going back to sleep. Would she hear painful moans coming from crumpled bodies, or would she see the wide-eyed stares of the dead?

"If they did survive, let's just say when they wake up they'll be wishing they hadn't." Her hand clutching the receiver trembled with fear. "Good night, Chad." She hung up before he could reply.

Chad pulled into the parking space next to Bridget's car and turned off his vehicle. She was at her flower shop, just as he'd thought she would be at this time of day. Last night's phone call had not only bothered him throughout the night, but all day long.

The hit-and-run was one thing, but Bridget herself had him concerned. She hadn't sounded like the Bridget he knew. The voice was the same, but the spirit was not. Something was upsetting her, and his gut told him it was more than the vision.

He studied the front window of The Garden of Eden as he crossed the parking lot. Attractive, classy, and colorful—all the qualities of the owner herself. A few well-placed-pumpkins, orange, red, and yellow silk leaves scattered about, and bright chrysanthe-mums let everyone know fall was here and Hallow-een was right around the corner.

A bell above the door sounded as he stepped into the shop. A middle-aged woman behind the counter glanced up and smiled. "Good afternoon. May I help you?"

Bridget's home had nothing on her shop. The Gar-den of Eden was nearly blinding in its brightness and color. Flowers and plants were everywhere. Since the shop was an end store, the side wall was practi-cally one huge pane of glass. Sunshine and overhead lights reflected off sparkling glass shelves and tables. A huge refrigerator unit containing what had to be every flower known to mankind filled the far wall. Ceramic and cloth grinning pumpkins competed for space with porcelain angels, stained glass boxes, and wreaths. If a person was looking for a gift, this was the place to come.

He pulled his gaze away from the shop and turned it to the woman behind the counter. "I would like to speak to Bridget Mackenzie, please."

The woman stopped placing pink long-stemmed roses into a crystal vase. "Perhaps there's something I could help you with?"

"It's personal." He noticed the gleam of specula-tion in the woman's eyes and had to wonder how many men walked into the shop asking to speak with Bridget.

The woman raised a brow and carefully lowered the rose in her hand to the counter. "I'll see if she's available."

"Thank you."

He turned away as the woman disappeared into the back of the shop. A ghostly trio of candles caught his eye and he was reminded that Mischief Night, or Devil's Night, would be coming up next month. Lord, how he hated it and the destruction that usually came with it. The soaping of windows or throwing of corn from his own youth was child's play to what kids did nowadays. Pumpkins were tossed through windows. Fires were set to empty buildings and warehouses. People could and did get hurt. It made no sense. Half the time he thought the whole world had gone crazy. The other half he knew it had.

"Chad?"

He turned at the sound of Bridget's voice. "Hi."

She looked very professional and fallish in dark green slacks and a gold sweater. Her hair was neatly styled and brushed back away from her face. Delicate gold and green earrings matched her necklace. A touch of expertly applied makeup would fool most people but didn't hide the truth from him. Bridget had spent one miserable night.

"I was on my way home from work and thought I'd stop in to see the place."

"Oh." Bridget waved a hand in the general direction of all the flowers. "This is it. As you can see, not a fig leaf in sight. The closest we come is the weeping fig tree over in that corner."

She hadn't believed him, and he hadn't expected her to. She knew where he lived and worked, and neither place was near the northeast section of the city. "I don't see any apples, either."

"We tempt our customers with flowers, not fruit."
Bridget smiled at the woman behind the counter.
"Why don't you knock off fifteen minutes early,
Mary? I'll close up."

Mary finished putting the last rose into the vase
and carried it to the refrigerator unit. "Sure. I'll be
out of here in a minute." Mary gave him a knowing
wink. "I know when I'm not wanted."

"Mary." Bridget's voice held exasperation.

"Yes?"

Bridget just sighed and shook her head. "Have a
nice night. I'll see you in the morning."

Mary slipped on her coat and grabbed her purse.
Her "Bye," was barely out of her mouth before the
door closed behind her.

He glanced away from the closed door and back
to Bridget.

She was frowning at him.

"Mary seems nice."

"She is. What happened?"

"What do you mean, what happened?" As far as
he could tell, she'd just let the help go home fifteen
minutes early.

"Did the hit-and-run occur? Do you have a lead
on your partner's killer?"

"Nothing happened, Bridget. There was no hit-
and-run reported last night and nothing new on
Mark's murder has come to light." He was relieved
to see her relax a bit. Showing up at her shop hadn't
been his brightest move.

"So why are you here?"

Good question. Excellent question. Why am I here? "I

thought if you didn't have any other plans, I could take you to dinner. I owe you a meal or two."

There, that hadn't sounded too desperate. A nice quiet dinner so he could assure himself she was okay, and then he was out of there. It was a nice safe plan.

"You worked off your dinner by helping me paint." Bridget gave him a questioning look. "If I accept your invitation, will I have to paint your living room in return?"

"No, you'll have to put up with my company for the next hour or so." She didn't look too upset with the prospect of painting his living room. Lord knew what color she would choose. Probably teal or something equally blinding.

"I guess I could handle that." Bridget glanced at her watch. "Give me about five minutes to close up shop here."

"Sure, take your time. I'll amuse myself by looking around." He purposely took himself to the other side of the shop and looked around. Being too close to Bridget had affected his thinking ability. He wasn't supposed to ask her to dinner. He was only going to check on her, to see for himself she was okay. One look at the dark circles under her eyes she was trying so valiantly to hide, and he was inviting her to dinner. Good Lord, what if the woman broke a fingernail or got a paper cut? He might actually propose to her.

Where was all the professionalism he prided himself on?

"Ready any time you are." Bridget stood by the

front door. She had pulled a blazer on over her sweater and was ready to go.

An hour later he pushed his empty plate to the side and silently groaned. Dinner had been great, but the company had been excellent.

Bridget was an exceptional woman. Most of the time his conversations with a female dinner companion fell apart around the time the salad was delivered. He just didn't have a whole bunch in common with the fairer sex.

Bridget was a different matter. There wasn't a topic they had hit upon that she didn't know something about, have an opinion on, or, at the very least, would listen to his opinions.

He had planned to stick to nice, safe neutral subjects like her shop, the weather, and even Philly's football team. They would have a nice dinner. He'd pick up the check and make sure she got home all right. No big deal. No stepping over any lines.

His plan lasted until the waitress delivered their drinks. Then somehow—and he still wasn't sure how—his plan got all mixed up. They talked politics over salads, religion and the death penalty over their entrées. While they hadn't agreed on everything, she made compelling arguments for her opinions and never once looked down on his views.

He had never enjoyed a dinner or a woman's company more, and that scared him to death.

The waitress stopped at their table and removed

the empty plates. "Would you like to see the dessert menu?"

He glanced questioningly at Bridget.

Bridget shook her head. "No, thank you. Dinner was excellent."

The waitress looked at him. "Just coffee." He glanced at Bridget. When she nodded, he added, "Make that two."

As the waitress disappeared through the maze of tables, he studied Bridget's face. Such a beautiful face, from the dancing of freckles across her nose to the generous mouth that made him think of warm nights and hot sex. Bridget's mouth was made for sin. It was her eyes that gave him pause—soft green eyes that had seen too much evil in the world, eyes that were surely older than her twenty-seven years.

Bridget's hand went up and brushed back her hair, making sure it was in place. "What's wrong?"

"You tell me." It was still with him, the feeling that something wasn't right. Even after an hour in her company where everything seemed fine, something was still wrong.

"What do you mean?"

"Something's wrong. I noticed it last night on the phone. What's bothering you?"

Bridget glanced away. "Nothing's wrong, Chad."

The waitress sat two cups of coffee in front of them and then rushed off to another table. He took a drink and sighed as Bridget avoided his eyes. "I've never known you to lie to me, Bridget. Why now?" God, why did it hurt to think she was lying to him?

"Who says I'm lying?"

"I do. It's in your eyes. Something is wrong and you're not telling me."

"That's not lying, Chad. It's withholding pieces of myself." Bridget's fingers tapped against the cup.

"It's lying by omission." He could see she was indecisive. "I know it's not about the case—or cases, as it may be. I think you've told me everything you know about that. It's something else. Please, won't you tell me so that I can help you?"

"You can't help. No one can help." Bridget's head was bent and she seemed to be studying the coffee in her cup.

"So tell me anyway."

Her soft green eyes swam with tears as she glanced up at him. "I can't take much more, Chad. I can't keep watching men die night after night and not go over the edge. I'm so tired of the whole thing, and I can't make it stop."

He reached for her hand and squeezed it. Her cold fingers trembled beneath his. "How can I help?"

"You can't. No one can." Bridget pulled her hand away. "I never should have dragged you into it again. You, me, we together, can't change the future. It will win every time." Huge tears clung to her dark lashes for a moment and then slowly rolled down her pale cheeks. Bridget impatiently brushed them away.

"Maybe, maybe not." They were tears of her soul. Bridget's soul was crying out and he didn't know how to answer. How did you comfort a person's soul? "I don't know the answers, Bridget. All I do know is if you stop fighting it and don't even try, it will win every time. It will eat at your soul until there's nothing left."

"Who says there's anything left now? Maybe I don't have a soul. Did you ever think of that? Maybe when I was cursed with the visions, my soul was taken in exchange. I'm nothing but a freak of nature. I don't have a soul."

"You have a soul, Bridget." He reached across the table and captured a tear with the end of his fingertip. "It's in your eyes and it's weeping."

Bridget's huge soft eyes stared at him for a long moment. Her sweet, moist lower lip trembled in the low lighting. Finally, on a weary sigh, she said, "I'll keep trying."

"I'll be there for you, every step of the way." His commitment came easily to his lips, easier still to his heart.

Fifteen minutes later he watched as Bridget let herself into her house. He had refused her invitation for coffee and turned down her offer of seeing the completed living room. He'd seen her confusion and made up some excuse about a meeting. They were holding another brainstorming session regarding Mark's murder down at the precinct, and he was planning on attending.

But the real reason he hadn't wanted to accompany Bridget into her home was he was scared. Yellow, chicken, flap-your-wings scared. He wanted to pull her into his arms and give her comfort so bad his mouth had gone dry and a deep burning ache had settled into his gut.

In the privacy of her home, there would have been

no stopping him. He would have taken her upstairs, made slow sweet love to her, and then held her all through the night. He would have been there when the vision came and went—just as he'd promised.

But was that the kind of comfort Bridget needed or even wanted? His previous relationships with women had been physically satisfying at best, emotionally distant at worst. The women he became involved with had known and accepted his terms. There had never been any emotional breakups or scenes. When one or the other had wanted the relationship to end, it ended—no broken promises, no broken hearts. Everyone went home happy.

Did he even have a home? No, what he had was an apartment, a place to hang his coat and throw his exhausted body across a bed. A place to watch a football game without being disturbed and take a shower when he was dirty.

He leaned against his car and watched as lights flicked on in different rooms of Bridget's house. Bridget didn't just have a house, she had a home.

The damned place welcomed him as soon as he crossed the threshold. It made him uneasy. At the same time, it made him feel warm inside. It made no sense, and until he could figure out why her cheery yellow kitchen made him want to put his feet up and enjoy a second cup of coffee, he didn't want to go back inside.

Oh, he wanted Bridget's body with a desperation that made him question his every motive where she was concerned, but she didn't play by the same rules he did.

Bridget was home, hearth, and, if she followed in her brothers' footsteps, a house full of babies. It was enough to give a confirmed bachelor nightmares and cold sweats. Bridget Erin Mackenzie came with a steep price tag, one that was way over his credit limit.

With one last look at her warm, beckoning home, he got back into his car and headed downtown for the meeting.

Bridget reached for the phone next to her bed and punched in Chad's number. She had it memorized.

For the past two nights, she had called Chad in the dead of the night and related any additional information she had gleaned from the visions that haunted her sleep.

It hadn't been much—the shape of the taillights; yes, it was a four-door sedan, dark blue or dark green, but not black; the duffel bag had Nike written on it; the sound of breaking glass, as if a headlight had been broken; the men's anguished cries as they went flying.

Tonight she had one more piece of the puzzle, the piece Chad had been waiting for. She glanced at the clock and was surprised to see it was nearly dawn. Usually the visions came upon her within an hour of falling asleep. Tonight they had waited. She wondered if it meant anything.

"Bridget?" Chad's voice didn't contain the rough edges of sleep.

"How did you know it was me? Did you get caller ID?" She was heartened to know no other crazy woman was calling him in the middle of the night, only psychopath Bridget and her fun-filled dreams.

"No. I've been waiting for your call."

"All night?" Since the visions of the hit-and-run started three nights ago, she had always awakened the poor man. She hadn't expected him to stay up tonight waiting for her call.

"No. I woke about three with the realization you hadn't called yet." Chad gave a deep yawn. "I was beginning to worry."

"Sorry about that. The vision didn't come until now." She leaned against the headboard and hugged a pillow to her chest. Shamrock, who was curled up into a ball at the foot of the bed, gave her an irritated look. Once again Shammy's sleep had been disturbed.

"Anything new?" Chad sounded disinterested, but she knew it was an act. Chad was very much interested.

"Yeah." She took a deep breath and gave him his lead. "It's the same killer."

"You're sure?" The disinterest was definitely gone from his voice now.

"As sure as I can be." Chad now had his lead on Mark's killer. How he was going to follow it, she hadn't a clue. The car could be a good place to start, but it probably was stolen.

"How do you know? Did you see anything? A face, a silhouette, anything at all?"

"No." She stared at Shamrock and wondered if

cats dreamed or had horrifying visions of the future. If they didn't and there was such a thing as reincarnation, she wanted to come back in her next life as a cat. "I felt it. The same hatred, the same insanity. Whoever it was wanted to run down those two particular men, but it's not his final goal. He's still playing a game, Chad. He's not done yet."

"Christ!"

"There's going to be more. I can feel it. The anger is getting stronger. It's feeding off his victories. It's giving him strength and power. He's starting to feel invincible."

She looked away from Shamrock and into the shadowy darkness of her bedroom. A chill slipped down her back and she hugged the pillow closer. "He's going to succeed, isn't he, Chad? You're not going to find him in time to stop those men from being run over, are you?"

All she got was silence on his end of the phone. She had her answer. "The visions aren't going to stop." She heard the tremor in her voice, but it didn't matter. Nothing mattered except making the visions stop. "They're going to keep coming until you stop him, Chad."

"I'm trying, Bridget."

She buried her face in the softness of the pillow. "I know. You're a good cop, Chad. I have faith in you. You'll stop him. Sooner or later, you'll stop him."

"I'm praying for sooner."

"So am I, Chad." She wondered where the sense of inevitability came from. Did it mean she had given up all hope of fighting the visions? She didn't know. All she knew was she was sitting here discussing two men's crippling injuries or deaths and there wasn't a tear in her eye. She had lost the ability to cry, and that scared her worse than the visions.

"Bridget?"

"Yeah?"

"What time do you get off work tonight?"

"Not till eight. Why?"

"I'll stop by around eight-thirty or nine, okay?"

Chad wanted to see her. Why was he always so full of contradictions? The other night he wouldn't even step in the house for coffee or to see what his handiwork had helped accomplish. Now he wanted to see her.

She wouldn't read too much into it. Chad probably only wanted to pick her brains about the visions. He had his connection now, and he'd run with that lead. "I'll be here." She lowered the pillow. "Good night, Chad."

"Bridget?"

"What?"

"Take a look outside. It's morning already." Chad's voice deepened to a rich baritone as smooth as expensive brandy. "Good morning, Bridget."

Chad hung up before she could respond. She placed the receiver back into the cradle and looked out the window. Chad had been right. Dawn had broken. From her second-story window, she could see the brilliant colors of the leaves on the giant oak tree in her front yard. Pale sunlight glistened off the morning condensation of each leaf, giving the entire tree a magical appearance. She wanted to smile at the sheer beauty of it, and yesterday she would have. She would have stood at the window and admired the precious gift Mother Nature had bestowed right in her front yard.

Today was a different matter. Today she had more important things on her mind than the colors of the leaves or the brilliance of the sun. Today she had lost the ability to cry.

SIX

At eleven o'clock that night, Bridget walked into the kitchen and turned off the coffeepot. Chad obviously wasn't coming. Something must have come up. She could only pray something had broken on the murder case of his partner, something solid that would lead to the arrest of the killer before he struck again.

Shamrock was patiently waiting at the patio door to be let back in after her evening exploration. Bridget opened the door and stood back as the cat strolled in. "Catch anything interesting?"

Shammy gave her a look that seemed to say, "Wouldn't you like to know?" and curled up on the rug in front of the doors to groom herself.

Bridget chuckled. "Well, I guess I've been put into my place."

The knocking on her front door had her hurrying into the living room. It had to be Chad. She crossed her fingers and hoped he had good news. She opened the door, took one look at his haggard face, and all her hopes came crashing down.

"What happened?"

Chad tossed his jacket at a chair and sank onto the couch. She closed the door and slowly sat at the other end.

Chad not only looked like hell, he was dressed like it. Chad didn't wear Armani, but he was usually dressed better than this. His black sweatpants had faded to a dingy gray from too many washings, his sneakers had a hole in them, but the sweatshirt with the ripped off sleeves was the crowning touch. She had to wonder if he had gone undercover as a street person.

Chad silently stared down at his sneakers for a long time and then buried his face in his hands. He gave a low mumbling sound, but she couldn't make out the words.

"What?" She was getting scared. She had never seen Chad act like this. She reached out and touched his arm as she looked him over from head to toe. He didn't appear physically hurt. "What happened?"

Chad lowered his hands and turned his head to look directly at her. "It happened, just like you said it would."

"The hit-and-run?"

"Yeah." The gold flecks in his eyes darkened and his eyes turned stormy. "Most Thursday nights a bunch of guys from the precinct get together and we shoot some hoops down at the elementary school on Ryan Street. Tonight was no exception. It was around seven-thirty, and I was already inside the gym playing in a game with some of the other guys. Dan and John were late, but there was nothing unusual in that."

"You knew them?" Another common denominator. First the same killer, now men Chad knew and worked with. They were all police officers.

"I've been working with Dan Bowers and John Hunt for six years now. They're both detectives down at the precinct." Chad buried his face back into his hands and pressed the heels of his palms against his eyes. "I should have known, Bridget. The parking lot, the duffel bag—everything fit except the coat. The coat with the Flyers emblem on it threw me. John and Dan don't like hockey. They're both football and basketball nuts."

"Who was wearing the jacket?"

"Dan. Tonight was his birthday. That's why they were late. Dan's wife talked John into coming in and having a piece of cake with the family. Dan's wife loves hockey and it's been a long-time joke down at the precinct how they fight over the remote at home and how they try to get the other one involved with their sport of choice. Dan's wife bought him a Flyers jacket and then had their five-year-old daughter give it to him as his birthday present. Dan had to wear the jacket tonight to please his daughter."

She held her silence as long as she could, and then she asked the question she had been dreading. "Did either one of them survive?"

"They both did." Chad's eyes were full of anguish when they met hers. "John's in serious but stable condition. He's pretty busted up, but the doctors seem confident he'll pull through okay."

"What about Dan?" She pictured her vision and realized now what all the joking and joshing had been about. John had been ribbing Dan about the jacket and possibly about his birthday and becoming another year older.

"Critical and in I.C.U., barely hanging on when I left the hospital. He was bleeding internally, and they had to go in to stop it. The doctors feel that went as well as could be expected with the amount of damage they found. They're more worried about his back. It's busted up pretty bad, and he's paralyzed. They won't know if it's permanent until all the swelling goes down."

Chad glanced away from her, but not before she saw the sheen of tears in his eyes.

"Hell, Bridget, they don't even know if he's going to make it through the night, let alone ever walk again."

She glanced at Chad's bare arm, where her own hand rested. What was she supposed to say? What could she say? Sorry just didn't cut it. She lowered her hand. Chad looked like he could use a few minutes alone. Without a word, she stood up and walked into the kitchen.

Shamrock gave her a sympathetic look as she walked into the room, but she didn't stop her primping. Cleanliness was very important to a cat, especially a vain cat.

Bridget glanced at the coffeepot, figured it was at least two hours old, and decided against a caffeine fix. She had enough trouble sleeping. Instead she sat at the table and with dry eyes stared at the flowers she had brought home tonight. A green vase overflowing with daisies sat in the middle of the table.

When she was younger, daisies had made her happy. They were simple and made her think of sunshine and summer days. Five years ago, when Chad had sent her a bouquet of daisies while she was in the hospital, they had made her cry. She had known they were his good-bye. Tonight they made her feel . . . absolutely nothing. She was numb inside. Her entire body felt frozen.

Where had all the tears gone?

Five minutes later, Chad joined her at the table. He appeared to have gotten himself back under control, but his first words slammed against her frozen senses. "How in the hell do you stand it?"

She stared at the white and yellow daisies as the numbness inside her vibrated. With enough vibration, would she shatter into pieces so small and numerous even all the king's horses and all the king's men would never put her together again?

Chad gave a weary sigh. "I shouldn't have asked that question, Bridget. Please forgive me."

"I don't mind questions, Chad, as long as I know the answers." She looked away from the flowers and studied the fatigue and curiosity lining Chad's face. Her fingers inched to smooth away his frown. She couldn't blame him for asking such a question. If the situation had been reversed, she might have asked it, too. How did she stand it? "Ask a simpler one."

"How old were you when you first had a vision?"

"Four. I dreamed my brother Sean broke his arm and that he was crying." She gave Chad a small, fleeting smile. He had looked appalled by her answer. "I drove my family nuts for three nights straight.

Only Sean, who was six at the time, could comfort me. On the fourth day, he fell out of the tree in the backyard and broke his arm. To this day, he swears he never cried, though."

"Didn't your family think it was strange?"

"Yes and no." She gave Chad a curious look. "Why haven't you asked me this before?"

Chad never had been interested in her past, only the current visions. Five years ago, he never questioned her about her abilities, where they came from, or how long she'd had them. He had been strictly professional through the whole ordeal. He had only been interested in the visions of a rapist.

"Maybe I wasn't ready to hear the answers."

"Now you are?"

"I'd like to think I am." Chad shoved his hand through his hair. "Before it didn't matter."

"Now it does?"

"It might."

The case! He's still thinking about Mark's death and the hit-and-run.

For one wild moment, she'd actually thought he might be taking a personal interest in her as a person, as a woman. Color her a fool. She had no idea how her past could help, but she'd answer his questions.

"My father was deeply concerned, while my mother seemed more accepting. That night Grandmom Rosalie came to see me. She stopped in and visited Sean for a while, but it was me she'd really come to see.

"Rosalie O'Hare is my mom's mom, and she has what she refers to as the sight or the gift."

"She's clairvoyant, too?" Chad seemed to accept this better than some members of the family. Having one clairvoyant in the family was strange. Having two was downright nerve-racking.

"Yes. I presumably inherited the curse from her side of the family."

"Why does she call it a gift and you call it a curse?"

"Grandmom Rosalie will tell you it's because I've never accepted it, and she has." A petal fell onto the table and she picked it up with the tip of her finger. Pieces of a flower. Pieces of her soul. "Grandmom is now seventy-two years old. She's seen the death of nearly every family member for the last sixty-some years, including her own husband's."

Chad shivered. "Why does she call it a gift?"

"She's tried to explain it to me more times than I care to remember. She says she had four days to say a private good-bye to the man she loved and was married to for forty-eight years. My grandfather suffered a massive heart attack while watching one of his grandsons' Little League games. He was dead before he hit the ground. Even if he had suffered the attack in an emergency room, they wouldn't have been able to save him."

"Why didn't she stop him from going?"

"By this time she had accepted the fact that the future couldn't be changed, no matter how hard or how desperately she wanted it to be." Lessons Bridget still couldn't accept. "Grandfather loved baseball almost as much as he loved his grandsons. She knew he would die doing something he loved. Not many people get that chance. Anyway, when the word reached her, she already knew and accepted it."

"It still doesn't make it a gift."

"I was old enough to argue that point, but her counterargument was just as good. When a loved one dies, especially unexpectedly like that, the grieving family always says they wish the person would come back, even if it's only for five extra minutes, just so they have a chance to say good-bye. My grandmother had four days for her good-bye."

Chad was silent for a long time before he spoke. "It's a compelling argument."

"Only if you believe the future can't be changed."

"That's what you haven't accepted yet. You still believe you can change the future, don't you?"

"If I didn't, I never would have gone to you and told you about the vision. I would have sat at home, read about Mark's death in the paper, and just accepted it."

Chad gave her a funny look. "But that's what happened anyway."

"No, I haven't *accepted* anything. I haven't accepted the fact that the visions are truth and nothing I do will change them." She rubbed the daisy petal between her finger and her thumb and watched as it rolled into a tight ball before crumbling apart. "The more I try and the more I fail, the easier it would be just to accept it. I don't think my grandmother saved herself any heartache, but I'm beginning to think it saved her sanity."

"Does your grandmother still get visions?"

"No, she says she's too old for visions. The dreams are like her eyesight. They've faded over the years. Nowadays she gets feelings in her sleep. If she starts fretting, the family goes into a panic."

"They don't call you?"

She looked away from Chad and over to Shamrock, who was now peacefully sleeping by the patio doors. "No. They know my visions stopped five years ago."

"You haven't told them they've returned?"

She shrugged as if it wasn't important. "None of the visions concern them."

"What about the visions in the past? Did they concern your family?"

"Always. Grandmom Rosalie says that's how the dreams work. You only see loved ones, family members. If we had visions on everyone, on everything, our sanity or our health wouldn't last a week."

"So why are you having visions about Mark, Dan, and John? They aren't your family or loved ones. You've never even met them."

"I don't know."

"What about five years ago? Why did you start to have dreams about the coeds being raped and beaten? You didn't know any of the students, so why them?"

"I don't know. It scared me so much that I risked looking like some lunatic and went to the police. I never had a vision that didn't involve my family, and none of the visions had ever been violent. It was a first, and it shook me pretty badly."

"It hasn't been your last, either."

"No, it hasn't. My grandmother thinks I started

to see the other coeds because eventually it all came back to me. She believes we can see our own future. She knew when she was going to miscarry once, but she wasn't sure if it was her future she was seeing or that of her unborn child."

Her grandmother also had another theory, one that was too embarrassing to tell Chad. Grandmom Rosalie had thought Bridget had been seeing Chad's future because he was destined to become the love of her life. Months after the incident, Rosalie'd had to admit maybe that theory hadn't been right, especially when Chad hadn't stopped around or even called.

"So why are you seeing the current visions?"

"I don't know, Chad. I don't even know why they started back up out of the blue. Five years of silence, and then one night, bam . . . your partner is being shot right in front of my eyes."

A flash of pain crossed Chad's eyes, and she regretted that insensitive statement. "Sorry, Chad. I didn't mean that the way it sounded. It's just that I've been wracking my brain for a connection. I can't find one to any member of my family or to myself."

She rubbed at her temples where a headache was beginning to form. "Five years ago, I had visions about young female college students who lived on campus. I matched that profile. It made sense. There was a connection. This doesn't make sense. The victims have been male and police officers. They're even out of the same precinct."

"There's one more connection."

"What?"

"I know them all."

"You think the killer is going to kill every person you've ever known?"

"No, but I'm a common denominator. I've worked with them all."

"So has every other officer down at that precinct." Why was Chad so insistent to pile all the blame on his own shoulders?

"I've been at every scene."

And you feel guilty as hell about it. "How many other officers were in that gym playing basketball tonight?"

"Seven." Chad pushed back his chair and stood up. "All from the precinct, too."

"The killer could be holding a grudge against the precinct and is out to get as many of the cops that work there as he can." Chad reminded her of a caged tiger in a zoo. He looked ready to pounce at the least provocation.

Chad paced across the kitchen, and then back. He stopped directly in front of her. "Listen, Bridget, I don't want you involved in this."

The words registered, but they didn't make any sense. She blinked up at him. Chad looked dead serious. "Excuse me?"

"I said I don't want you involved in any of this, Bridget. It's too dangerous. There are too many unanswered questions. You could get hurt."

"How precisely am I to become uninvolved?" Chad wasn't making any sense. "I know! How about if I stop having the visions? Gee, that was simple. I don't know why I didn't think of that before."

"Okay, so you can't just shut off the visions."

Chad paced to the other side of the room, careful not to disturb Shamrock. Contradictions again. Chad looked frustrated enough to rip steel bars off any cage with his bare hands, yet he noticed and was thoughtful enough not to disturb her sleeping cat.

"I could stop telling you about them." She didn't like the almost hopeful expression on his face. "But that would mean I would have to sit back and just accept the future and whatever it held. I don't know if I'm ready for that, Chad. It's this damned Irish stubbornness running through my blood. It won't let me just sit back and accept fate."

Chad paced to the other end of the room. He appeared to be thinking, and thinking hard.

"I guess I could find someone else to call in the middle of the night. Problem with that is not too many people would believe me. Even if they did, they wouldn't have your resources as a detective to pull it all together and make sense of it all. What I need is a cop who's open minded, hopefully into the new age approach to life, and has your resources and intelligence. Anyone down at the precinct fit that description?"

She couldn't prevent the sarcasm that dripped from her every word. Chad was getting her upset. What did he mean he didn't want her involved? How could she not be involved? She stood up and moved into the living room. The vase of daisies was too tempting, and his head too big.

Chad followed her into the room. "Bridget . . ."

She picked up his brown leather jacket and held

it out to him. "I'm sorry for calling you. I won't do it again. Consider me totally uninvolved."

"You haven't listened to a single word I've said, Bridget." Chad took his jacket and put it on.

"Yes, I have. You said you didn't want me involved in this." She took several steps back. Chad was beginning to get angry, and that made her uneasy. After what happened to her five years ago, big, strong, angry men terrified her. Chad didn't terrify her, but he definitely made her uneasy. Why would he be angry with her? He was the one who'd told her to back off.

"I also said it was too damned dangerous." Chad stalked her across the room.

She backed up until the arm of the couch dug into her thigh. "I feel no connection between the killer and me. This doesn't involve me, Chad. I'm not in any danger."

"You just told me you only have visions concerning family members and yourself. We already ruled out family members, so that leaves you."

"I said *in the past* the visions only centered around family and loved ones. I don't know about these visions, Chad. My grandmother has never known anyone who had been blessed with this gift who had it taken away. When I lost the ability to have the visions five years ago, it changed the rules. No one knows these rules."

Chad advanced until he was mere inches away from her. She could feel the heat of his body and see the thunderous pulse beating in his neck. There was a certain hunger in his eyes, a hunger her body responded to. The uneasiness she had felt moments before melted away. She relaxed against the arm of the couch and met his intense stare head on.

"I can't chance it, Bridget." Chad stepped closer and the inches disappeared. His rock-hard thighs pressed against her softer ones. He seemed to be struggling with every breath he took. His warm brown eyes turned heavy with promises that would have terrified her coming from any other man.

She pressed closer and felt the shudder that rocked his chest. Her breasts were suddenly full and wanting his touch.

"Why can't you chance it, Chad?" For the first time in five years she wanted to chance a lot of things, and every one of them had to do with this man.

Strong hands gripped her shoulders and hauled her closer still. "Because you are beginning to mean too damned much to me." His mouth took possession of hers before she could form a reply or even a coherent thought.

The kiss wasn't gentle or tentative. Chad kissed like a man who had been denied the pleasure of a woman's lips for eternity. He captured. He took. He conquered.

Bridget wrapped her arms around his neck and matched him every step of the way. Teeth nipped at kiss-swollen lips and tongues mated to the rhythm of their straining bodies and pounding hearts.

Heat coiled tightly in her abdomen as Chad's hands cupped her bottom and pressed her tightly against the front of his pants. The junction of her thighs cradled the hard column of his arousal. Liquid desire pooled beneath the barrier of her jeans and satin panties. She wanted Chad with a swiftness and ferocity that would have shaken her if she hadn't felt his answering response.

Chad broke away from her lips and trailed a path of open-mouthed kisses down the side of her neck. She buried her fingers deep in his hair as he licked her skin and gently nipped at her pounding pulse. Her nipples puckered in anticipation against the lace of her bra. She arched her throat to give him better access, and whispered his name in a soft plea.

Chad's tongue was tracing the faint scar marring her throat when he suddenly released her.

She would have fallen if she hadn't landed on the arm of the couch. She blinked in surprise. Chad stared down at her as if he had never seen her before. Pure panic filled his eyes, but his gaze never once left the scar encircling her throat.

"Oh, hell, Bridget." Chad took a deep breath and three steps back. His breathing was fast and harsh. It matched hers perfectly. "That shouldn't have happened." He took the few remaining steps to the door. "That definitely shouldn't have happened."

Chad opened the door, looked outside onto the porch, and then back at her. He clearly wanted to say something. What, she hadn't a clue. All he did was shake his head and step out onto the porch. Before he closed the door behind him, he gave her one more look she couldn't decipher and said, "Lock the door behind me, and buy yourself a damned dog."

She sat there and stared at the closed door for a good five minutes after she heard Chad drive away. She had her answer. Chad's kisses didn't repulse or frighten her. They made her yearn. They made her burn. For the first time in five years, she felt safe in a man's arms. She felt alive. She felt frustrated and edgy.

A soft female smile curved her mouth as she locked the door and turned off the porch lights. Chad hadn't been unaffected by that kiss. She had felt his arousal, hot and heavy, pressing against her thighs. He had wanted her—at least for a moment he had, until his lips touched the scar encircling her throat. The reminder of their past.

Her smile slowly faded as she continued to turn off lights and lock up for the evening. How did a person fight the past while trying to change the future?

Chad frowned at the computer monitor in front of him. Nothing. In the two days since the hit-and-run, the entire precinct had come up with nothing solid. Everyone was working ungodly hours and the media was crawling out of the woodwork.

The only good news they received was that John was improving daily and was expected to make a full recovery. Dan, on the other hand, wasn't improving, but he wasn't getting any worse. Dan would have to die to get worse. There was still no word on the paralysis, and the doctors had to go back in and remove his spleen when it had ruptured late the previous night.

The monitor beeped, and he gave it the command to go to the next case. This was the second time he had been through these files, but the first time hadn't produced the results he wanted. He was trying to cross-reference any case that Mark, Dan, and John had worked on together. There were quite a few, but nothing jumped out at him as a possible lead. The few that had held possibilities turned out to be dead ends.

The task force investigating Mark's death had been expanded to look into the hit-and-run. The only connection between the two incidents had been that the victims were all officers working out of the same precinct.

As long as they were open and actively seeking connections between the two cases, he didn't feel compelled to mention Bridget's role in all this. There wasn't a man on the task force who wouldn't laugh his butt off as soon as he mentioned a clairvoyant had foretold both incidents. They would love the part where she just "knew" the shooter and the driver were the same person.

He had a feeling they wouldn't be laughing when she predicted this was all a game to the killer, that the killing wasn't over yet.

Chad closed his eyes and pinched the bridge of his nose. The screen in front of him was beginning to blur. In his mind, thirty was awfully young to be investing in reading glasses. He should turn off the machine and hit the streets to follow up on their one solid clue.

The car that had plowed into Dan and John had been a '90 Ford Taurus, dark blue. It now had damage to the front end, particularly the driver's side. The headlight had been smashed, and by the amount of damage done to Dan and John, it was safe to assume there had to be more than a few crinkles put in the hood and possibly the fenders. Body shops throughout the city were being advised to be on the lookout for such a car.

Last week a car matching that description had been reported stolen in Bryn Mawr. Over the last year, another two had been stolen in the surrounding area. They hadn't gotten the report back from New Jersey yet. With bridges connecting Philadelphia to New Jersey, they couldn't rule out the possibility the vehicle was from out of state. Pay a toll, do a crime. Too many possibilities and too many places to look. Bridget hadn't seen the license plate to give him a number or two, let alone tell if it had been an out-of-state plate.

Their one lead was slowly drying up before their eyes.

"Hey, Barnett, you got a visitor!"

His swivel chair creaked as he turned around and faced the reception area to the squad room. Bridget stood there, seemingly unaware of the small commotion her presence had caused. She was too busy looking at every man and woman in the room. A few younger officers were straining their necks to get a better look, and being quite obvious about it. A few older, more mature officers cast an admiring glance before going back to whatever they had been doing. Most were busy glancing speculatively back and forth between him and Bridget. In all the years he'd worked there, never once had a woman come to see him on personal business. Every cop in the room took one look at Bridget and knew it had to be personal.

How the hell was he going to explain Bridget? His best course of action was not to explain her at all.

With a weary sigh, he stood up and headed for the reception area. Today she was wearing a dark green blazer, an orange top that should have clashed with her red hair but didn't, and a flowing skirt that came to mid calf and consisted of every fall color known to mankind. A touch of gold jewelry winked delicately at her ears and around her neck.

How was it possible for Bridget to become more beautiful, more desirable in just two days' time? He might not have seen or talked to her since the night he had lost all his senses and kissed her, but she hadn't been out of his mind since.

He approached her and couldn't contain his frown as she ignored him to continue to glance around the squad room, smiling at everyone she saw. His voice was a low whisper. "Bridget, what are you doing here?"

A few of the cops had been around five years ago when Bridget had become quite a topic of conversation in the squad room. Beautiful twenty-two year-old clairvoyant coeds hadn't been the norm back then. In fact, there hadn't been one before or since. He didn't want any of the older officers who hadn't recognized her to connect this gorgeous woman to that coed, so he kept his voice low. Bridget wasn't that common a name, and it might jar someone's memory.

Bridget gave him a quick glance and then returned her attention to the glass-partitioned offices on the far side of the room. "Shh . . . I'm concentrating."

He shuddered to think what she might be concentrating on. He prayed it wasn't another vision. "Come on."

He grabbed her elbow and escorted her through a maze of desks to an empty office. He closed the door and was tempted to close the blinds as well, but refrained. He could feel at least five pairs of curious eyes boring into his back.

Bridget looked past his shoulder to a bank of desks to the left. She hadn't once met his gaze.

He looked away from her mouth and the heaven it could deliver. "What are you concentrating on?"

"Faces." Bridget moved to the left to get a better view.

"I might regret asking this, but why?"

Bridget gave him a look that clearly stated her opinion of his intelligence. "If I have any more visions concerning the cops in this precinct, I might be able to put a name to the face or faces." A frown marred her brow as a young detective walked by the office. "Well, not a name, since I haven't been introduced to them, but I'll be able to describe them to you better."

"I thought I told you I don't want you involved in this." Frustrated, he ran his hand over the back of his neck and gave her his toughest glare, one Mark had sworn made criminals shudder during interrogations. It didn't seem to faze Bridget at all.

"I am involved. I can't become uninvolved, as much as you would like me to." Bridget smiled pleasantly at another officer walking by. "I figured the best thing I can do is give you the most accurate information I can." Her soft green eyes had hardened with determination—or was it pure stubbornness? "If I had met your partner before the shooting, I might have recognized him enough to tell you who was going to be shot. I might have also recognized Dan Bowers and John Hunt."

"You might not have. Didn't you say it was too dark to see them clearly?"

"That's correct, I might not have. But one thing I do know. If I don't see or meet the people during my waking hours, I'll never be given the chance to recognize them in the visions." Bridget finally pulled her attention away from the squad room beyond the glass walls and stared stubbornly back at him. "Either I tell you or I tell someone else, Chad. But I will tell."

Chad leaned against the door and closed his eyes. He'd lost and she had won. It was that simple. Bridget was bound and determined to stay involved, and there was nothing he could say or do to change her mind. Either she came to him with what she knew, or she would go to someone else.

He opened his eyes and looked out over the squad room. He would trust his life to just about everyone there. They were good, honest cops who fought the unending uphill battle for justice with him every day. There wasn't one he would trust with Bridget's life.

Call it conceit, arrogance, or just plain pigheadedness, but there was only one man for this job, and he was that man.

He turned and faced Bridget. "We do this my way, and only my way."

Bridget's smile stretched from ear to ear. "Yes, Chad. Anything you say, Chad."

He didn't believe her. She was agreeing too readily to terms she knew nothing about. "I'll remind you you said that later."

"I'm sure you will." Bridget's smile never faded.

He wanted to taste that smile, wanted to back her up against the nearest wall and sink into her warmth. His arms might ache to pull her close and pick up where they had left off the other night, but his body throbbed and burned. The scary part of the whole thing was it wasn't just sex. Sex he could handle either by taking a cold shower or by taking Bridget to bed. What he was feeling for Bridget was more than just lust.

The thought of failing her again brought an acid burning sensation to his gut. The idea she could be hurt by this latest wave of visions filled him with pure terror. The warm, vibrant colors of her home felt too damned comfortable for his jaded soul. He was even beginning to like her contemptuous cat.

But it was the kiss they had shared that had shaken him to the bottom of his soul and captured his heart.

Bridget kissed like eternity.

SEVEN

Bridget turned onto her street and groaned. Chad's car was parked in front of her house. Of all the nights for Chad to get off at a decent hour, why did it have to be tonight? She glanced in the rearview mirror at her brother's pickup truck, directly behind her.

Dillon had surprised her by showing up at the shop half an hour before it closed. It seemed Grandmom Rosalie was fretting up a storm and her worries centered around Bridget. Dillon, who'd been lucky enough to have the day off, was elected to drive to Philly and bring Bridget back to her hometown of Reading.

She wasn't going back to Reading with Dillon, and he wasn't accepting her assurances she was fine and nothing bad was going to happen. Dillon had left the shop, picked up a bucket of chicken for their dinner, and followed her from the shop to her home. The argument with Dillon hadn't really begun yet, and now she had Chad to contend with on top of everything else.

She knew why the family had volunteered Dillon for this assignment. Her tears didn't sway Dillon, who was four years older than she and a Reading city fire-fighter. Brian, who was partners with their brother Sean in a construction company, also was immune to his sister's tears. Sean and Connor were pushovers when it came to their baby sister or any other woman who had learned from an early age that a few tears could get a woman her way. Being the baby sister of four overprotective brothers who wouldn't allow her to tag along and do any neat stuff with them, Bridget had learned to cry to get her way. She wasn't proud of that, but if the trick worked, she wasn't above using it.

With Dillon, tears weren't going to work. She was going to have to use logic.

She turned into her driveway. Chad was sitting in one of the rockers on the porch. Her heart gave a funny little lurch at such a domestic scene. He looked so relaxed and carefree sitting there slowly rocking back and forth, enjoying the evening air—at least until Dillon pulled in right behind her. Chad's gaze shifted to the truck and its occupant and didn't budge. With a weary sigh for the battle that was yet to be fought, she got out of the car and waited for her brother.

Dillon gave Chad a curious glance before joining Bridget on the walk and giving her an inquiring one.

She shrugged. "Friend." She had a better chance at hitting the lottery than at Dillon's not connecting this Chad Barnett to the detective from five years before. Chad hadn't met her family back then, but his name was familiar to them all.

She stepped up on the porch and mustered a friendly smile for Chad. "Hi, you're early."

The last two nights, since her unexpected visit to the precinct, Chad had dropped by to check on her. He usually showed up around nine and was gone before ten. He never stayed for coffee or even a glass of water. He never repeated the kiss. He had been nothing but courteous and professional. Chad was driving her crazy.

"You're busy." Chad never took his gaze off Dillon as he stood up.

"No." As her brother cleared his throat, she quickly added, "I mean yes, kind of." She nervously jiggled her keys. "Chad, I'd like you to meet one of my brothers, Dillon." She waved her hand at Chad. "Dillon, I'd like you to meet Chad."

Dillon shifted both bags of takeout food to one hand and stretched his other toward Chad. "Sorry for barging in like this unannounced, but sometimes Bridget is hard to pin down."

Chad reached for Dillon's hand. "No problem. As she said, I'm early."

Dillon's gaze was glued to the gun Chad was wearing under his jacket. "I'm figuring cop, right?"

"Detective. Detective Chad Barnett."

Bridget's heart dropped as she inserted the key into the lock. It was over now. Any second Dillon was going to throw her over his shoulder in some fancy fireman's carry, toss her into his truck, and not stop driving until they reached the Reading city limits. Considering Chad's attitude for the past few days, he'd probably offer to feed Shamrock while she was gone.

"The same Detective Barnett?" Dillon's voice had deepened.

"The same."

Bridget shoved open the door, flipped on the light, and started to babble frantically. "Well, what are we all standing on the porch for? Come on in and see how the living room turned out, Dillon."

Dillon nodded at her. "In a second, sis." He turned back to Chad. "Thanks."

Chad raised an eyebrow. "For what?"

"Shooting that bastard." Dillon gave him a frustrated smile. "It would have helped more if you'd done it a day earlier."

"Four weeks earlier would have been better still." Chad looked away from her and her brother.

Bridget's heart swelled with the love she felt for Dillon and for the rest of her family. They had been there with unconditional love and support when she had needed them. It had been especially hard on her brothers to see her like that, knowing what had happened. Her brothers had protected her all her life. When she had been beaten, raped, and nearly choked to death, they felt as if they had failed her in some way. It had taken quite a while to convince them they hadn't. They couldn't protect her from the cruelties of life unless they took away her pleasures, too. She hadn't been—nor was she—willing to live like that.

As for Chad, her heart went out to him. She knew he still believed he'd failed not only her, but the other coeds, too. The first rape happened four weeks to the day before her own. Frank Barelli's spree of terror had lasted twenty-eight nights.

"Are you guys coming in or what?" She didn't want to remember the past tonight, and she surely didn't want Dillon and Chad dwelling on it. It would just give them more ammunition for the argument yet to come. "Chad, you'll stay for dinner, won't you? I'm sure Dillon picked up enough food to feed his platoon back at the station."

Chad and Dillon entered the house and closed the door behind them. Dillon shoved the bags into Chad's hands. "Of course he'll stay. There's plenty to go around. It's only fried chicken and a couple of side dishes."

Her brother slowly surveyed the living room. "Hey, this turned out real nice. Brian and Connor did a good job on the floor."

"Chad helped me paint it." She smiled at Chad. "You'll be happy to know he didn't think living rooms should be painted pink, either."

"I thought it was Iced Raspberry." Chad shrugged and glanced around the room as if seeing it for the first time. "I'll have to admit it turned out a lot nicer than I thought it would."

"That's the problem with men. They have no imagination." She waved her hand at the room. "Anyone with any imagination at all would have known this room had been crying out for Iced Raspberry. Just like the dining room is shouting for green, moss green." She gave both men a superior look before heading into the kitchen.

* * *

They were halfway through the meal when Chad's curiosity got the best of him. "So, Dillon, what brings you to Philly? Business?" He knew Dillon was a fire-fighter back in Reading, but he might have business with Philadelphia's Fire Department. It was one of the best in the state.

"I came to see if I could talk Bridget into taking a short vacation back in Reading."

Chad glanced at Bridget, who was studying the chicken bone on her plate as if it contained valuable DNA information. Something was up. Every instinct he'd developed over the years was starting to scream.

"Ah, you need a babysitter. Bridget told me about your unusual but practical solution to getting things done around here and giving you and your brothers some quality time with your wives."

"Well"—Dillon looked sheepish—"I wasn't plan-ning on hitting her up on the babysitting until some-time in February. I've got some time off then, and I was hoping to surprise Allison with one of those Caribbean cruises for Christmas."

Bridget smiled at Dillon. "You'd better book your babysitter now, because Connor was mentioning something about Aspen in February."

She finally looked at Chad. "My dad had to go to Germany for a year on business. Mom wasn't about to let him go without her, so my babysitting services will probably triple in the next eleven months. I fig-ure by the time my parents come home next August, my house will be completely done."

"So why vacation back home if your parents aren't there?"

"Well, it's not really a vacation. Grandmom Rosalie has been asking to see Bridget." Dillon heaped more cole slaw on his plate, along with another corn biscuit.

"The same Grandmom that frets up a storm when a family member is in trouble?" Chad stared at Bridget, but she wouldn't look at him. Now he knew why his instincts were screaming.

"The same." Dillon glanced between Chad and his sister. "I can't seem to convince her to come, though."

"I have a business to run, Dillon." Bridget stood up and carried her plate over to the sink. "I can't leave it just because Grandmom is worrying."

Chad slowly smiled. It was the perfect solution to get Bridget uninvolved—park her butt back in Reading under the watchful eyes of her brothers until Mark's murderer was caught. "Your employees could handle it."

Dillon looked at him and returned his smile. He had found himself an ally.

"Yes, my employees could handle it. I trained them all. But I'm not going. I'm perfectly fine here. There's no danger to me."

"Yet!" Chad knew Dillon and the rest of her family had no idea her visions had returned. It was about time they did. "Just because you haven't felt danger to yourself yet in one of your visions doesn't mean it won't happen."

Dillon nearly choked on a mouthful of biscuit.

"They're back! Why the hell haven't you told us, Bridget?"

Bridget shrugged and rinsed her plate in the sink. "There was no reason to. No one back in Reading was in any danger."

Dillon stood up and walked toward his sister. "Who exactly *was* in danger?"

"A cop." Bridget glanced over her shoulder and spared Chad a pained look. "I mean cops. One's dead and two are in the hospital."

"The cop that was shot in the alley over a week ago?" Dillon stared at his sister as if trying to piece it all together.

"Yes. The other two were involved in a hit-and-run last Thursday night." Bridget walked over to the table and started to put everything away.

"They're not your usual visions." Dillon looked at him. "What about you? Weren't you able to help?"

"The cop who was shot was Mark Monterey. He was my partner, and I was half a block away picking up some coffee when it happened. The two involved in the hit-and-run were also from my precinct. Seven other cops and I were in the building next to the parking lot where it happened, playing basketball. Bridget's convinced both crimes were committed by the same person." He could see the concern on Dillon's face and couldn't blame him. His sister was having visions of a killer. "I've been trying to get her to back away from these cases as much as possible. I don't want her involved. So far no one else but me—and now you—knows she is."

"I'm gathering she's not cooperating." Dillon

stared at his sister with such a look Chad almost felt sorry for her. Almost.

"She's right in this room and *she* can speak for herself." Bridget stared right back at her brother. "Listen, Dillon, I love you and every other member of the family, but I'm not going back with you. Grandmom Rosalie is probably picking up the stress I've been under lately because the visions have returned. Chad will tell you I haven't picked up one feeling, one inkling, one anything that tells me I'm in danger. The victims all have been male and detectives at the same precinct. Chad's the only one who knows about the visions and he hasn't told anyone, not even his superior officer. As long as the investigators are handling both crimes as if they might be connected, there's no reason for him to mention me. What's he going to say? Some clairvoyant who hasn't had a clairvoyant thought in five years thinks both crimes were done by the same person?"

Dillon glanced at Chad. "What's your take on this?"

"I'll tell you what his take should be." Bridget crossed her arms and tapped the toe of her shoe on the tile floor. "The only one in this room who's at risk is Chad. He's the one who fits the profile, not me."

Chad heard the concern in her voice and almost smiled. When was the last time anyone had been concerned for him? Hell, when had anybody *ever* been concerned for him? "I can take care of myself, Bridget. It's you I'm concerned about."

"Since there's nothing in the recent visions to warrant your concern, I guess I have to assume it's because of the past. Our past." Bridget stood there and literally dared him to deny it.

He couldn't. "I can't deny the truth, Bridget." His gaze landed on the thin white scar encircling her throat. That scar had haunted every dream he'd had since Bridget walked back into his life. It was a constant reminder of his failure to protect her. "The past will always be there. We can't forget it."

"No, but some of us would like to get over it. Five years is a long time to wallow in it, Chad. I managed to allow it to ruin my life for two years. I didn't go out after dark and if I had to, I was never alone. I didn't date. I didn't so much as step into an elevator if the only other occupant was a man. I wore turtlenecks and scarves for two years straight, even on the hottest days of summer."

"What happened?"

"I figured out Frank Barelli and his sick twisted mind was still victimizing me every day of my life. I'd kept him alive and breathing with my fear. I couldn't allow it to continue."

Bridget looked at her brother and smiled. "I took a couple of self-defense courses. No, I can't kill anyone with my bare hands and I'm not even a black belt. But I can cause some major pain if the situation arises.

"I forced myself to go out into the night and realized there wasn't a boogey man hiding behind every tree. I stopped covering the scar and stopped worrying about what other people thought of it. I've even gone out on quite a few dates."

"All admirable, Bridget, but you're still scared." Chad had seen the pain and fear still lurking in her eyes. He should have been able to prevent it from ever entering them.

"It's called being cautious, Chad. Only a fool wouldn't be alert after what I've been through. I still sleep with a can of Mace under my pillow, and there's always a can of pepper spray in my purse and my coat pocket. I lock doors behind me and have a high-tech security system at the shop that's directly linked to the police station. I've made sure every one of my sisters-in-law and my mother took self-defense courses. Grandmom Rosalie opted for a gun instead because of her bad hips."

"You're kidding!" A seventy-two-year-old Irish great-grandmother packing heat! It was enough to give every cop in the state an ulcer. He glared at Dillon, who was chuckling.

"I was kidding about the gun, Chad." Bridget laughed right along with her brother. "She does have some difficulties with her hips, but nothing that will keep her down. We bought her an Irish setter named Ferguson. He's trained to disable a person, but you'd never know it to look at him. Grandmom puts big green bows in his hair to keep it out of his eyes and won't let him outside in the cold without a doggie sweater."

He shuddered at the image. "Fine. You're cautious, your whole family is cautious, and granny's living with a cartoon. It doesn't change the fact you should go back to Reading with Dillon. Give me a phone number and I'll call you as soon as we apprehend the killer." Shamrock rubbed against his leg and he reached down to scratch behind her ears.

Bridget kept her arms crossed. "For the last time, I'm not going anywhere. My home is here. My business is here. If I thought for one moment my going back with my brother would change anything, I would. The visions would still come, and you'd be sixty miles away instead of seven."

Dillon finally decided to join the conversation. "Have you had a recent one, sis?"

"Not since the hit-and-run, and that happened a week ago." Bridget walked toward Dillon and gently cupped his cheek. "I love you, Dillon, but I'm not going back with you. Grandmom Rosalie will understand."

"She already said you wouldn't come, but I had to try." Dillon pressed his cheek against her palm. "Promise to call if you need anything."

"Yours will be the first number I dial."

"Promise to listen to and obey Chad. He seems to know what he's talking about."

"I promise to listen, but the obey part is a little shaky." Bridget glanced over her shoulder at Chad and rolled her eyes.

Dillon chuckled. "You're going to make some man a miserable wife."

"If I recall correctly, Allison had that word stricken from your wedding vows. It went something like love, honor, and cherish."

Dillon tapped her nose and then kissed it. "Stubborn."

The love between brother and sister was tangible.

Chad wondered what it would have been like to have a sister to love, someone who was family.

Dillon walked over to him, and Chad stood to shake the man's hand. "Take care of her."

"I'm trying." It would be a hell of a lot easier if she just went home with her brother. He hadn't taken very good care of her five years ago, but neither Bridget nor her brother seemed to hold that against him.

Dillon pulled a piece of paper out of his pocket and started to write. Two minutes later he handed the paper to Chad. "Call any number on this paper if she gives you a hard time."

He glanced at the list. All four brothers' home phone numbers were listed, plus Connor's pub, the fire station, and the construction office Sean and Brian owned. "What, no Grandmom Rosalie's number?"

Dillon chuckled as he pulled on his jacket. "Don't worry. She'll know you're in trouble before you do."

Chad watched as Bridget walked her brother to the front porch and envied their closeness. Even with sixty miles between them, they were still close. Dillon seemed like a nice enough guy.

When Dillon's pickup had pulled in behind Bridget's car earlier, he'd been surprised. The obvious conclusion had been that Bridget was bringing home a date. He'd been shocked at his reaction. His initial response had been to deck the date, drag Bridget up to her bedroom, and make love to her until there wasn't a doubt left in her mind that she was his.

Bridget was his. What an unsettling thought that

was. No one was his. He didn't have a possessive bone in his body—at least he hadn't until Bridget came knocking on his apartment door. If he was honest with himself, he'd have to admit he wanted Bridget.

The kiss the other night had been a huge mistake. Not only had it given him a taste of paradise, it had shown him his feelings toward Bridget weren't professional in the least. He wanted her with an intensity that rattled his soul.

"Dillon's off." Bridget stepped into the kitchen. "Now you've seen what I have to put up with. I love my family dearly, but sometimes they can be a real pain."

"I think he meant well." He scraped his plate and loaded it into the dishwasher.

"Locking me in some ivory tower and throwing away the key is meaning well. Driving sixty miles on a hopeless mission when he should be home with his wife and two little girls is pushing it." Bridget opened the back door and let Shamrock out. "He knew I wouldn't go back with him before he even came."

"I say that's love."

"I call it overprotective."

"Maybe it's one and the same." He glanced around the kitchen and realized there was nothing left for him to put away. "It looks like I owe you another dinner."

Bridget shook her head. "Not me. Dillon." She walked out of the room, led the way to the couch, and sat. "Can I ask you a personal question?"

He sat down at the other end, putting as much

distance between them as the floral cushions would allow. "What?"

"Why did you become a cop?" Bridget kicked off her shoes and pulled her legs up under her. "I'm sure there are plenty of other jobs out there you could do. Most probably even pay better."

"How do you know what being a cop pays?" He wasn't sure if he wanted to answer her original question or not.

"Dillon always says the two most underpaid careers are firefighter and policeman."

"So why's your brother a firefighter?" He couldn't argue with that wisdom.

"Dillon's always had a fascination with fires. When he was a little boy he used to sit in front of the station a few blocks away from our house. When the trucks rolled out of the bay doors, he'd follow them on his bike and would sit for hours watching them fight fires. Dad always said Dillon would be either a firefighter or an arsonist. We're just happy it turned out this way." Bridget took off her earrings and tossed them onto the coffee table. "Did you follow cops around?"

He wondered what else she was going to take off. "No. I was taught to fear the cops—that they were bad and if they found my mom, they would take her away from me."

"Who told you that?"

He saw the near hero worship in Bridget's eyes and wanted to put an end to it before it even began. "My mother."

He couldn't picture her face, but other memories

of his mother were still there—stringy bleached blond hair that never seemed to be combed, thin arms that never held him, huge sobbing coming from behind the locked bathroom door as his mother vomited what little food she might have eaten.

"My mom wasn't your typical mom. She was a junkie and had a couple of convictions for prostitution. I came home from school one day and found her dead on the bathroom floor from an overdose."

"How old were you?"

"Seven." The hero worship was gone, replaced by sympathy. That was just as bad. "I asked a neighbor to call the police. They couldn't take her away from me now. The guy up the street who sold her the drugs did that for them. While I waited for the police to arrive I made a promise to myself to take the people who sold the drugs off the streets so other little boys didn't lose their moms. To do that, I became what my mother feared. I became a cop."

"A very good one, at that."

"It's never good enough, Bridget. For every criminal you take off the street, there's four more to take his place." He noticed the space between them wasn't as great as it had been a moment before.

"Imagine what it would be like if there weren't any cops, let alone good ones." Bridget shifted her weight and managed to move five inches closer to him in the process. "Can I ask another question?"

"This seems to be the night for it." The light floral scent of her perfume was driving him crazy. He'd noticed it earlier in the kitchen, but now it haunted him. He wanted to discover every spot on her body where she had dabbed it.

"Why haven't you married, or at least found a significant other?" Bridget's soft green eyes seemed to churn with hidden mysteries.

"Besides not having found Mrs. Right?" He hadn't been looking for Mrs. Right or even a Ms. Right. If a woman he met fit that category, he headed the other direction as fast as his legs would carry him. He wasn't the fastest sprinter in the academy for nothing. So why wasn't he running now?

"Besides that."

"Cops make extremely bad husbands. Terrible hours, lousy pay, constant danger, and we usually have rotten days. No one ever calls us to report a good deed or to say someone left a hundred-dollar bill in their mailbox. It's usually a dead body, a trashed apartment, or dear old Uncle Horace swinging from the rafters. It doesn't make for stimulating conversation over the meatloaf and mashed potatoes when the *little woman* asks you how your day went and to pass the gravy."

Bridget chuckled.

"You find that funny?" He always figured Bridget's sense of humor was a little off kilter, but this was pushing it, even for her.

"No, Chad, I find it sad." The smile slipped from her face. "We're a bunch of misfits—the cop and the clairvoyant. What a pair we make. You'll be discussing your latest homicide case and I'll be telling my meatloaf partner not to go near Roosevelt Boulevard today because I keep having visions of a jackknifed tractor trailer sitting on top of his spiffy new minivan."

"Ouch, that hurt." He couldn't stand to see the pain in her eyes, so he smiled and teased. "A spiffy new minivan. Must be hell seeing the future."

Bridget threw the pillow sitting next to her at his head. He caught it with one hand and grinned. She looked adorable with that green fire blazing in her eyes. The space between them was nearly nonexistent. He reached out and tenderly brushed a wave of her hair behind her ear and out of her eyes. The auburn silk wrapped around his finger. "Well, Miss Clairvoyant, if you're that good at seeing the future, tell me what I'm going to do now."

Bridget's gaze fell to his mouth. Heat coiled in his gut and desire raced to his groin. He lost the ability to breathe when the tip of her tongue streaked across her lower lip, leaving behind a glistening trail of moisture.

"You're going to kiss me." Bridget whispered, her voice trembling. "You're going to kiss me like a man would kiss a woman he wants."

He leaned in closer and cupped her cheek. His roughened palm caressed her warm, smooth skin. Would the rest of her feel this soft, this silky?

"Is that what I'm going to do?" He raised his gaze from her tempting mouth to her eyes. They were no longer soft green. They had darkened to the color of summer grass. Hunger and fire burned in their depths.

This was insanity. He shouldn't be doing this, but he couldn't stop now. This attraction was too powerful to be one-sided. He needed to know if Bridget was feeling it, too.

"Do you want me to kiss you?"

"More than I want my next breath." Bridget wrapped her arms around his neck and raised her mouth to his.

It was more than any sane man could refuse. He captured her sweet offering in a kiss meant to be slow and tender, but which quickly turned wild and taking. With Bridget, there was no control, no safety net of chivalry. The hunger that flared between them burned it all away.

His tongue claimed possession of her mouth as her hands pulled him closer. Heat exploded and desires raged as the kiss deepened and hands explored. Their legs tangled as the cushions cradled their weight. Moans mixed with sighs and he was unsure and uncaring who was doing what.

She covered his face with tiny kisses and her even white teeth nipped delicately at his ear. His hand slipped under her top and skimmed across the warm flesh of her stomach. At her sigh of pleasure, he cupped one of her breasts with his palm. Her bounty overflowed his hand, her hardened nipple pressing against the lace of her bra. Bridget arched farther into his hand and captured his mouth with a kiss meant to shatter what was left of his control. She almost succeeded.

The clothes between them became a barrier to his sanity. What the hell was he doing? He'd meant to kiss her, nothing more. He removed his hand from under her top and carefully smoothed the blouse back down over her stomach. Not half an hour ago, he'd promised her brother he would take care of her. He didn't think Dillon had this in mind.

His breathing was harsh and irregular. It matched hers. He ran a hand through his hair as he sat back up and pulled her into a sitting position beside him. He took a deep breath, prayed for strength, and looked into her eyes.

Hunger, confusion, and perhaps embarrassment swirled in the soft green depths. Hunger he knew how to handle. He'd take her upstairs and make love to her until all that was left was satisfaction. The confusion he sympathized with. No one could be more confused than he was at this moment. It was the embarrassment that tugged at his heart and conscience.

"Remind me never to kiss you while I'm wearing my gun." He had taken off his sports jacket and holster earlier. They were hanging on the back of a kitchen chair.

"Why?"

"With all the heat we generate, the bullets would probably go off and I'll be lucky if the only appendage I lose is a toe." He shuddered to think what else he might lose in the heat of the moment.

Bridget softly smiled. "Yeah, I can see where that might be a problem." The look of embarrassment had left her eyes, replaced by what appeared to be anticipation. Bridget was obviously looking forward to their next kiss. So was he, but it wasn't going to be tonight. His control was frayed to its limits.

If he kissed her one more time, there would be no going back. They would christen her newly decorated living room in a way that would have every one of her brothers driving to Philly toting a shotgun.

Hours later, Bridget was pulled from an erotic dream of Chad by the smell of smoke. She pushed the smell aside and burrowed deeper under the covers. She was just coming to the good part, where Chad finally turned all her frustration into glorious satisfaction. Black swirls of smoke started to obscure Chad.

She fought the vision that was intruding on her dream. It was a senseless battle. The vision would come, as it always did. But something about this vision terrified her. The thick black smoke swirled and danced until it surrounded her, choking off all the air she needed to breathe.

Tears stung her eyes. Suddenly there was a wall of flames as high as she could see. The smoke was gone. In its place were bright flames licking at everything in their path. Their red, orange, and yellow blinded her. Blue streaks of pure energy shot through them and devoured everything. The fire was feeding and growing like a living beast.

She tried desperately to see what was in its path, what it was feeding on, but wall after wall of flames surrounded her. As they fed, they roared and thundered so loud she had to clasp her hands over her ears to block the sound.

And then she heard it. Over the roaring inferno,

she heard the high-pitched scream of a woman calling for help.

Bridget jerked awake, fell out of bed, and knelt on the floor, gasping for air. Tears streaked down her face, and her heart pounded faster than the flames that had consumed their fuel. She coughed and choked and prayed for the burning sensation in her lungs to subside. It was as if she had been caught in the inferno. It had been so real she could still feel the heat against her face. Shamrock curled into her lap as she rested her head against the side of the bed. To get up would take too much energy.

When the coughing eased, she reached for the phone and brought it down next to her. She dialed Chad's number from memory. He picked up on the second ring.

"Bridget?"

"Fire."

"What! Where? Are you all right?"

She heard the panic in his voice, but she couldn't reassure him this time. She didn't have any clues except a faint woman's scream. "Fire, Chad. The killer is going to use fire."

She hugged Shamrock as she quietly replaced the receiver in its cradle and stared into the darkness of her room. When was it all going to end? How much more did she have to endure?

EIGHT

At the sound of tinkling bells, Bridget forced a pleasant smile on her mouth and glanced up to welcome the customer. Her strained smile faded when she realized it was Chad.

After the phone call she had placed to him last night, she had been expecting him, or at least a phone call from him, all day. She just didn't know what to tell him. There was nothing to the vision except a wall of flames and the faint sound of a woman screaming for help. She didn't want to tell him this vision scared her more than the other two combined.

Fire. What was it about that wall of flames that terrified her so? She knew a little bit about fire, thanks to Dillon. She also had a very healthy respect for it as a potential killer. There were four smoke detectors in her house and two in the shop. She changed their batteries every time daylight savings time kicked in or out and the clocks all had to be changed. Dillon had even given her a fire extinguisher for Christmas two years ago, and she kept it under the kitchen sink. So why couldn't she shake the image of consuming flames and thick smoke from her mind?

Chad glanced around the empty shop and slowly approached the counter. "You almost done for the night?"

She was passing the time by wiping down the counter. The glass doors to the refrigerated units next to her gleamed under the overhead lighting from her recent polishing. Short of spit shining the floors, there wasn't a whole lot left for her to do.

"We close in two minutes, and then I can knock off for the night." She straightened the rack of assorted note cards that usually got tucked inside an arrangement or plant.

Mary had handled the majority of the customers today while she had concentrated on receiving and organizing the flowers for the Steed wedding taking place Saturday. Tomorrow and Saturday morning would be hectic, arranging all those flowers. They'd also be extremely profitable. If Julia Steed equated a long happy marriage by the amount of flowers at the ceremony and reception, she was destined to celebrate a seventy-fifth wedding anniversary.

She glanced at Chad, who was studying an old wooden birdhouse complete with a blue-feathered bird peeking out and surrounded by ivy. He was giving it the same look most men who accompanied their wives into the shop gave it. The look clearly said *why would anyone want that in their home, let alone pay good money for it?* She hid her smile. She sold, on the average, two of them a week. "What brings you by?"

"Escort service."

"I thought that was illegal." She had to wonder what Chad would charge for such a service. The way he had kissed her last night, it couldn't be enough.

"Wrong kind." Chad glanced out the window to the parking lot beyond. "You have plans for the evening?"

"No, but I'm not really up to any, either. It's been a long day, and all I want to do is put my feet up and relax." She didn't have to tell Chad she hadn't gotten any more sleep after one-thirty this morning. One look at her and he and anyone else would know.

"Sounds good to me. How about if I follow you home and then call your favorite pizza delivery boy? I'm sure he could use the tip money to pay his tickets."

"You think he's been ticketed by now?"

"If not, I'm having him pick out some lottery numbers, because he's one lucky fellow." Chad leaned across the counter and tenderly touched her cheek. "You're looking like hell."

"You know how to make a girl's knees go weak."

"It's not your knees I'm worried about."

She raised a brow. "I'm beginning to see why you never managed to find Mrs. Right. Do those sweet words just roll off your tongue, or do you have to think about them first?"

"I'm a cop, Bridget. Sweet words aren't in my vocabulary. I tend to stick to the truth because it doesn't get me into too much trouble."

"So what you're really saying is I look like hell."

Chad ran a hand through his short hair and glared. "You know you're a beautiful woman,

Bridget. You don't need me to tell you that." Chad shifted his weight and asked, "Do you have a VCR at home?"

She blinked at the sudden change in topic. "Thank you, and yes, why?" *He thinks I'm beautiful!*

"There's a video rental place next door. How about if I go pick up a movie?"

"Sounds like a nice relaxing evening." She had to wonder at the startling change in Chad. Pizza and a movie didn't sound like a professional evening discussing clairvoyant visions.

Chad opened the door and was halfway out when he turned and asked, "Do you have any preferences?"

At least he cared enough to ask. She figured with his background, they were going to end up watching some cop movie or some high-speed adventure that would keep her on the edge of her seat all night. "Anything but *Back Draft* or *Towering Inferno.*"

Chad gave her a hard-eyed glare before walking away. The glass door swung shut behind him.

Two and a half hours later she leaned back on the couch and watched the ending of the Harrison Ford movie *Seven Nights, Six Days.* She had been pleasantly surprised by Chad's choice. Had he picked the romantic comedy for her, or did a romantic soul beat under that tough cop exterior? Her money would be on the latter. He had always been full of contradictions. Why not in this, too?

There was only one slice of pizza left in the box.

Half a bag of chips and four empty beer bottles littered her coffee table. Thankfully Chad wasn't the type of person who insisted on talking the whole time the movie played, just an occasional "pass the chips" and "do you want another one" when he had gone into the kitchen for their second beers.

She had to smile as the final scene played out and Harrison got the girl—as if there had been any doubt. She picked up the remote and hit the mute button and then the rewind button. "I must admit, Chad, you have excellent taste in movies."

"I figured I couldn't go wrong with Harrison. The man doesn't know how to make a bad movie."

Chad looked as relaxed as she felt. His jacket and holster were hung on the brass coatrack by the front door. He'd kicked off his shoes and propped his feet on the edge of the coffee table. Somewhere between the video store and her house, his tie had disappeared. He didn't look like hell. He looked like heaven in a six-foot package.

She leaned her head back and glanced at the pillow sitting between them. It was the same pillow she had tried to clobber him with last night. She was tempted to pick it up and try it again. But would she get the same heated results?

For now, she'd bide her time. She wanted some answers first. "Has anything happened I don't know about?" She could see where the phone call last night might have concerned Chad, but it didn't warrant escort, video, and pizza service.

"No, why?"

"Seems strange, your showing up at the shop just to see me home."

"Maybe I was concerned."

He had to throw that maybe in there. "Concerned about what? It wasn't like I never had a vision before."

"You sounded different last night, and you hung up before I could ask you any questions."

She wondered if she should tell Chad she had been choking on the smoke and her lungs had felt as if they were going to burst. "It wasn't very pleasant."

"I can imagine."

If anyone else had said that, she wouldn't have believed him. Chad was different. He might actually be the only person who could imagine what she went through. Even Grandmom Rosalie wouldn't have understood. Grandmom never visualized violent acts against young women or saw someone's brain get splattered against a brick wall. She shrugged and looked over at the television when the VCR clicked off. "I was upset, that's all."

Chad put his hands behind his head and leaned back farther into the cushions. "Want to talk about it?"

"No, but I will."

The sheen of interest in his eyes told her he was a lot more concerned than his relaxed appearance suggested.

"There was smoke, a lot of dark, swirling, dense smoke. Then a wall of flames erupted before my eyes. It seemed to surround me, growing angrier and larger as it fed, crackling and roaring so loud I had to cover my ears. Heat was everywhere, scorching me. Then I heard faint screams. It sounded like a woman's voice shouting for help."

"That's it?"

"That's it." She glanced at the pillow she was hugging. She didn't even remember picking it up.

"Okay, let's start with the basics. Was the fire inside or outside?"

"I don't know." The game of twenty questions had begun. Cop questions she would need to remember so she could look for answers the next time the vision came. "I couldn't see beyond the wall of flames. The smoke obscured everything."

"You didn't see anyone or anything besides smoke and flames? No furniture, no trees? What about a car? Could it have been a car fire?"

"Nothing. I vaguely heard a high-pitched scream, but hell, Chad, that could have been my own cry I heard." She hugged the pillow closer and pressed her cheek against its softness. "I just don't know anymore."

Chad straightened up on the couch and gave her his full attention. "What do you mean your own cry? Could you be the one who's trapped in the fire?"

She tried to cover her own shiver, but failed. "No, I meant my real scream as the vision was happening. I not only saw the fire and heard its roar, I felt its heat, Chad. I woke up choking on the smoke and shielding my face from the intense heat. I could have very easily been screaming in my sleep." She could name a hundred ways she would rather die than to be burned alive in such a fiery hell—from old age, say at ninety-two, was number one on her list.

Chad braced his elbows on his knees, cupped his chin in the palms of his hands, and studied the blank television screen. "I want you to go live with Dillon or one of your other brothers for a while."

"No." She'd known the subject would come up again. "I don't feel it was a threat to me, Chad."

"Who do you feel it was a threat to?" Chad held her gaze. "Do you feel it's the same person?"

She shrugged. "I couldn't tell during the vision. Logic would tell me it has to be the same offender, but that's logic talking, not the vision."

"So he's going to strike again, and this time he'll use fire."

"My guess would be yes."

"What about a time period? You had visions of the other crimes, what, four, five times before they happened."

"Yes, but there's no guarantee it would hold true on this one. Clairvoyance isn't a science, Chad. In fact, scientists usually laugh at it."

"They wouldn't if they could see what's happening now."

"Yes, they would. They'd come up with dozens of logical reasons for what I dream, pull in charts and percentages of chance and Lord knows what all else to discredit me. Failing all that, they'd turn up their Harvard-educated noses, declare me a fraud, a charlatan, or a voodoo queen, and back away as fast as their Ph.D. feet would carry them. In my experience, people tend to be afraid of what they don't understand." She gave Chad a small smile. She could tell he wanted to deny every word she had just said, but couldn't.

"Look what happened five years ago. The police had documentation of every one of my visions well before the actual rapes. Everything I said was going to happen happened." She took a deep breath and told herself Frank Barelli could no longer hurt her. "Even my own beating and rape. What happened after Barelli was stopped? Did anyone say, 'Gee, there must be something to this clairvoyant stuff?'192 No, most said if I were that clairvoyant I would have known what was going to happen and stopped it. A few even had a different theory, didn't they, Chad?"

She saw him blanch, but continued anyway. "They figured since I was feeding Barelli information on the coeds who were going to be attacked, he used my descriptions to pick them out. When I went so far as to convince you something was going to happen to me and you set me up in that apartment away from the campus, Barelli had no other option but to come after me. In other words, there were plenty of cops down at the precinct who thought I asked for everything I got."

"I'd been hoping you didn't know about that." Chad leaned back and rubbed at his temples. "There weren't plenty of cops who thought that, Bridget. Only a few. They changed their minds later on."

"With persuasion?"

Chad glanced at her from the corner of his eye. "Yeah."

She smiled. "What did that cost you?" There

wasn't a doubt in her mind who had done the persuading. Chad had once again charged to her rescue. She tossed the pillow aside.

"Under the circumstances, with Frank's death and all, I only received a reprimand in my file." Chad raised his eyebrow with interest as she moved in closer.

Her smile grew more confident. "I think you deserve to be properly thanked for that."

Chad's glance slid down the length of her body as she covered the remaining distance between them. "How proper?"

She leaned forward and placed a chaste kiss on his cheek. "Was that proper enough?"

He gave her a disappointed look and shook his head.

She placed a quick kiss on the corner of his mouth. "Better?"

This time Chad rolled his eyes before shaking his head.

"Okay, big boy, pucker up. You're about to be properly thanked." She intended to plant a big one on him and pull back before he came to his senses. This new freedom of expressing herself with a man was glorious. She wanted to savor every moment. The shadows from the past couldn't harm her here, not with Chad. She lowered her head and kissed him as he had kissed her last night.

A moment later she realized she'd been wrong. She was the one losing her senses. Chad had wrapped his hand around the back of her neck, and he wasn't letting her go. Nor did she want him to.

The kiss exploded with sizzling heat and burning desire. She wanted Chad's touch. She yearned for the feel of his hands caressing her body. She wanted to learn every inch of his body by sight, feel, and taste. She wanted to wrap her legs around his lean hips and feel the pleasure only he could give her.

She wanted to be a full woman again—to know love, to taste love, and to be loved.

Only Chad could give her that. Only his touch let her feel the desire instead of the fear. When he was near, she trembled with anticipation instead of terror. Her body had known all along what her heart was just discovering. She was falling in love with Chad.

She was half sprawled on top of him. His demanding mouth took everything she had to give, and she wanted to give more, so much more. She flattened her palm against his chest and marveled at the fierce pounding of his heart. It matched her own. Her mouth left his to trail a path of kisses over his jaw and to his ear. She nipped at his earlobe, then lightly ran her tongue over the spot her teeth had just teased. A shudder shook Chad's body and she smiled. He wasn't immune to her touch.

Chad groaned, gently cupped her face, and gazed at her with such heated emotion she nearly dissolved into a puddle of need. The gold flecks in his brown eyes blazed with hunger.

"We can't do this, Bridget." Chad's voice seemed to be scraping jagged glass.

She blinked in confusion. That wasn't what she wanted to hear, not tonight, not now when she wanted him so badly she was ready to chuck whatever self-respect she had and beg. "Why?"

"Lord, Bridget, don't look at me like that." His thumbs stroked her cheeks. "It's not that I don't want to. If you ever believe one thing about me, believe I want to make love to you more than I've ever wanted anything in my life."

"But you're not going to, are you?" The honesty burning in his eyes told her he was speaking the truth. Chad did want her as much as she wanted him.

"No." His tender kiss landed on the corner of her mouth. "I can't protect you if I'm in your bed."

"Protect me from what? I'm not the one in danger, Chad. You might be."

"The last time you didn't think you were in danger, either, but you were." The tip of one of his fingers traced the scar at the base of her throat. "One minute later, Bridget, and you wouldn't have been alive."

"This isn't like the last time, Chad." She closed her eyes and silently prayed the past wouldn't ruin the future. There was something special happening between them, and she wasn't going to allow the past to destroy it.

"You're right. This isn't like the last time. This is worse, much worse. There's a killer on the loose and people are dying, Bridget." Passion, truth, and fear rippled in his voice. "I can't fail you again."

She shook her head and placed a quick kiss in the center of one of his palms. "You never failed me, Chad."

How was she ever to convince him of that? He

might not have saved her body from the cruel hands and twisted sick soul of Barelli, but he had saved her from certain death. Chad Barnett had been her hero and savior once, but that was because destiny allowed it for no other reason than the whim of fate. Whatever the outcome of her current visions, there was one thing for certain. Fate would decide the conclusion. Grandmom Rosalie was right all along. What was to be, would be.

"If we become lovers, Bridget, the distraction could cost one of us our life." He covered her mouth with a series of small, quick kisses. "I'm willing to take that chance with my life, but I won't risk yours." For a moment, his kiss was deeper, longer. "No matter how tempting your pout."

"I never pout."

Chad nipped and pulled at her lower lip as she sighed with pleasure.

He chuckled a little unsteadily and gently lifted her off his body and onto the cushion next to him. "Then it must be the freckles that drive me crazy."

"Now you really are pushing your luck." She frowned as he stood up, stretched, and slipped his feet into his shoes. He looked like he was getting ready to leave. If she couldn't get Chad into her bed, she wanted him on the couch.

"No, we're pushing our luck if I stay any longer." His strong hand grabbed hers and he pulled her to her feet. "I want you to get some rest tonight."

"Easier said than done." She followed him to the door and watched as he strapped on his gun. "Do you want me to call tonight if the vision returns?"

She didn't know why she said *if.* It would reappear as surely as her brother Connor would serve green beer on St. Patrick's Day.

"Only call if you want to talk about it or if you see anything that might be useful." He kissed the tip of her nose. "If you can go back to sleep, do it. I'll take you to lunch tomorrow and you can tell me about it then."

"Lunch on a Friday?"

"I start the four-to-twelve shift tomorrow. I won't be able to stop by at night till next Wednesday."

"You're starting a new shift without a day off?"

"Yesterday and today were my days off." Chad shrugged into his jacket. "I visited Dan and John in the hospital. John's going to be released in two days and Dan's starting to improve. The good news is he's not paralyzed permanently. The swelling around his spinal cord is going down and he's starting to get some feeling back."

"That's great." The killer hadn't won that round. She would pray for the same results when the fire struck.

"He's not out of the woods yet, but it's starting to look better."

"I'm glad."

Chad leaned down and kissed her. "So am I." He kissed her again. "Good night and lock up tight."

She scrunched up her nose. "You're beginning to sound like one of my brothers, Chad."

"Knew I liked them for some reason." As if against his will, he pulled her into his arms and kissed her until she forgot how to breathe.

Chad broke the kiss with a gruff command. "Now get some sleep."

Then he was gone.

At one-thirty Monday morning Bridget fought the smoke as it threatened to block her dream—her wonderful dream. She was reliving the hours she had spent with Chad and his heated kisses good-bye. She wanted to fall back into the day and make sure it never ended. But the smoke kept getting in her way.

She waved her arms to clear the smoke just as Chad laughed at one of her corny jokes. She loved his rich, deep laugh. He laughed so seldom that when he did, it became a precious gift. Today Chad had given her that gift and she wanted to press it against her heart as she slept.

For the past two nights, the vision had basically remained the same. Smoke, flames, and the faint woman's screams that weren't hers. There would be a woman trapped behind the flames, but it wouldn't be her. Last night she was able to tell Chad it was going to take place inside a building. A deep, smoke-induced cough pulled her from the sweet dream of Chad and right into the hellish nightmare of the vision.

Flames erupted before her eyes and dense smoke rolled along a ceiling. A long narrow corridor of flames opened up before her. She was in a hallway! She was moving down the hallway, blocking her face from the heat and choking. What precious air she could breathe was thick and hot, scorching her lungs. Behind a wall of flames she could make out the outline of a door. Three brass numbers were nailed to the wooden door and gleamed a bluish color from the intense heat. Three-o-one.

Farther down the hall, on the opposite side, another door was being devoured by the flames. The numbers three-o-two shone blue and green through the fire.

Fear clutched at her throat as the next door came into view. Three-o-three!

She knew this place. This was the hallway she had walked the night she knocked on Chad's door and brought him into her living hell. Chad's apartment was number three-o-five!

The fire grew vicious and deadly. It closed in all around her. She couldn't get to Chad's door! Flames licked at her fingers and arms. She had to reach Chad!

Then she heard it. Behind the door marked three-o-three came the faint, weak screams of an elderly woman calling for help. She reached through the flames and grabbed the glowing doorknob. The pain branded into her palm and ripped a scream from her own throat that pulled her from the vision.

Bridget tumbled from her bed, clutching her burning hand and trying to reach for the phone. She had to warn Chad!

She punched out his number and cursed when she heard the busy signal. She slammed the phone back into its cradle and ran to the bathroom. Two seconds later, she had cold water pouring over her burning palm. There wasn't a mark on it, but the freezing water felt so darned good. She held her hand under the water and tried to think. What should she do?

She wrapped her hand in a towel and raced back to the phone. After hearing the busy signal yet again, she yanked a pair of jeans on over the shorts of her pajamas and raced downstairs.

Within two minutes, she was in her car and heading for Chad's apartment building. Twelve minutes later her worst fear materialized before her eyes. Fire trucks, police cars, and ambulances surrounded Chad's building. Flames were shooting from nearly every window on the third floor. Water arched through the air, men shouted, more approaching sirens wailed. She parked in the first spot she could find, grabbed her keys, and ran.

She couldn't get near the building and she couldn't see Chad in the chaos surrounding it, so she pushed and shoved her way through the mob of curious onlookers until she reached the yellow plastic police tape. The man standing next to her looked over and asked, "Just get here?"

"Yes." She glanced around the horde of people packed around her like sardines. They were pointing, talking, and some seemed to be making jokes. Most were in pajamas and robes. One lady had her hair in curlers and fluffy cow slippers on her feet.

Bridget wondered if there was a certain etiquette one must follow while gawking at other people's suffering. If there was, she was about to break the rules. She tugged on the man's sleeve. "Excuse me, but do you know if anyone was hurt, or"—she couldn't voice her worst fear—"missing?"

"No fatalities reported yet, if that's what you're asking, missy." He sounded almost disappointed that body bags weren't being carried out by the truckload. His massive chest seemed to expand with importance. Someone was asking him questions. "You missed all the excitement. Pretty calm now. Some people were injured when they had to jump from their third-floor balconies. Ambulances already took them away. Some smashed legs and an arm or two. I think there was even a compound fracture, but nothing serious."

She tried to swallow the lump of fear that had formed in her throat. The man was wearing blue paisley print pajamas, white sweat socks, and corduroy slippers. He talked about broken bones as if he were an orthopedic surgeon putting three kids through college.

"Everyone on the third floor had to be rescued off their balconies and there was some pretty exciting times before the trucks showed up. Some idiot on the third floor pulled a John Wayne number and smashed in his neighbor's patio door to rescue her. Heard she was some elderly woman who had a hard time walking and used a wheelchair."

Chad! That sounds like something he would do. Could the woman be the same one trapped inside three-o-three? It made sense. She would have been Chad's neighbor. "Could you tell me where this idiot might be?" She still couldn't spot Chad.

"My guess would be in the back of one of the ambulances, sucking down oxygen."

"Thank you." She saw two ambulances parked off

to the side, but in the darkness and shadows she couldn't see Chad. She turned and pushed her way toward the ambulances, muttering her apologies for stepping on toes and slippers the whole way.

Chad took a few steps away from the back of the ambulance and coughed up what felt like a third of a lung. He prayed it would be the last of the smoke he had inhaled. He pulled the blanket draped around his shoulders closer as he walked back to the ambulance and accepted the oxygen mask from the paramedic. A dozen Band-Aids covered the soles of his feet from where he'd had to walk over the broken glass of Mrs. Saleski's patio door.

"So, Barnett, can you add anything else?" He didn't know the cop taking his statement and was sick of answering the same questions over and over again.

"No, that's about it." He sat back down on the rear bumper and sucked in fresh, pure oxygen. "I'll call it in to my precinct and let them know what happened."

"Strange how the killer warned you with that phone call and all."

"Yeah. I'm one lucky guy." Chad went into a spasm as his lungs struggled to accept the cool oxygen. He'd thought breathing the smoke in was bad when he went into Mrs. Saleski's apartment to rescue her, but it had been a picnic compared to getting it all out of his lungs.

Mrs. Saleski was already at the nearest hospital being treated for smoke inhalation. They weren't taking any chances with her seventy-six-year-old lungs. The paramedics had wanted him to go along with her, just to be on the safe side. He'd opted not to. He had more important things to do than lie around in some bed getting poked and prodded.

The killer had made his next move, just as Bridget had predicted. He didn't need the fire chief to tell him how the fire started. The smell of gasoline that permeated the whole building told the story.

The killer had waltzed into his building, dumped five gallons of gas along the hallway of the third floor—if the empty can the fire department had found had been full—and struck a match. Bam! Instant inferno that could have killed every resident on the third floor and possibly some from the second and first floors.

Except this time the killer had called to warn him. Why? He'd been asleep for nearly an hour when the phone rang. He thought it was Bridget, even said her name when he picked it up.

It hadn't been Bridget. It had been a mechanical voice saying '*Liar, liar, pants on fire. Nose as long as a telephone wire.*'

The word *fire* had him jumping out of bed and flipping on lights as the phone went dead. Before his eyes could adjust to the sudden brightness, the smoke detectors in the hall started to screech. He punched out 911, gave the location of the fire, and moved.

The front door of his apartment already had smoke pouring in under it, and he knew enough not to open it. That left the balcony. He was wearing only his underwear, and he didn't stop to pull on pants or a shirt. He grabbed his gun, which was sitting on the nightstand, and headed for the balcony. The killer might have thought it would have been a howl to pick him off as he ran from a burning building.

Other people were pouring out onto their balconies, shouting at the residents from the first floor for help. Bridget's vision came back to him then. Bridget had heard a weak, frail woman's voice calling for help. Mrs. Saleski was the only elderly woman on his floor and she lived right next door. She wasn't on the balcony and her patio doors weren't open. He glanced at the six-foot space between his balcony and hers and then listened. No sirens were approaching. He had no choice. He couldn't allow Mrs. Saleski to perish because of him. The killer wanted him, not some elderly woman.

With his holster strapped over his naked chest, he'd stood on the railing of his balcony and done his best Tarzan imitation, without the vine. One skinned knee and what promised to be a wicked black and blue mark on his forearm had been his reward, along with a locked sliding door. Mrs. Saleski didn't answer his pounding or shouting. With a mighty swing of a metal plant stand she had on the balcony, he had shattered the tempered glass door.

He hadn't been sure what upset Mrs. Saleski more—smoke filling her apartment, flames starting to consume her living-room carpeting, the deafening roar of the fire, or the near-naked man smashing in her patio door.

It had taken him a precious moment to reassure her who he was, because she didn't have on her glasses. She had managed to get herself out of bed and into her wheelchair. With great care, he picked up the frail, trembling, and coughing woman and headed for the balcony. Fresh air hit their faces just as the first fire truck pulled into the parking lot.

Half an hour after he passed his frail burden to a fireman and climbed down to safety, he was trying to figure out how to get to Bridget's. He wanted to hold her, to reassure her the killer hadn't claimed another victim.

His car was blocked in by what appeared to be half of Philly's fire department. Even if it hadn't been, it wouldn't have done him any good. His keys were in the process of being melted to silver blobs. He was fashionably dressed in navy blue pinstriped boxers, a borrowed blanket, and an assortment of Band-Aids. Everything he owned except his police revolver and car was gone. He had spotted the flames shooting out his bedroom window and the patio doors. Nothing would be left.

But he was alive, and he had to wonder why. Did the killer misjudge the speed of the fire? Was the taunting telephone call supposed to be the last thing he ever heard before being overcome with smoke and dying? Or had the killer timed it perfectly, giving him enough time to escape but lose everything he owned?

The sudden quiet around him penetrated his thinking. He glanced up and looked directly at Bridget. She was standing five feet in front of him, just staring at him. Reflections from portable lights that had been set up shone in her eyes, obscuring her emotions. By the trembling of her arms as she hugged herself, he could gauge what they might be. She had had the vision again tonight and had probably seen enough to recognize his apartment building's hallway. He pictured her frantically calling him, only to get a busy signal. He hadn't hung up the phone after dialing 911. She'd driven through the darkened city to warn him, only to find her nightmare had come true.

God, what she must have lived through. He'd had to survive the fire only once, and that was enough for any person. Bridget had survived it night after night. She woke up choking on the smoke and hearing Mrs. Saleski's frail calls for help.

He removed the oxygen mask, and, without looking at the paramedic, handed it to him. He stood up and held out his arms and waited. Bridget raced into his arms and clung to him as if she would never let go.

He closed his eyes and pulled her closer. Nothing in his life had ever felt so good.

NINE

At four-thirty Monday morning, Bridget had Chad just where she wanted him—in her bedroom. Only problem was, she wasn't with him. To be more accurate, he was in the master bathroom connected to her bedroom, not in her bed. She leaned against the kitchen counter and slowly sipped a cup of herbal tea. Somewhere above her head the shower was turned off.

Her fingers trembled against the cup. Chad could have died tonight! She took another sip and a deep breath to ease the panic squeezing her chest. Chad was fine. Not only fine, he was a hero for saving Mrs. Saleski. The only injuries she had detected on his body were a bunch of small cuts to the soles of his feet and a scraped knee. Not bad, considering what he had gone through. But he could have died so easily.

She couldn't shake that terrifying thought. Chad could have been killed. The man she loved could have died in that fire. She wasn't falling in love with Chad, she was in love with him. When she'd spotted him sitting on the bumper of the ambulance with a plastic oxygen mask on, she knew she had fallen completely in love, plain and simple. No fireworks, no trumpets blaring. He had just been sitting there with a blanket wrapped around him and his bony, adorable knees and toes showing. She'd stood there for a full minute just staring at him before he realized she was there. When he stood and silently opened his arms to her, she ran into his embrace and stayed there.

She had been totally embarrassed when, a minute later, Chad had stepped back to break the hug. She'd been so terrified that her relief on seeing him blocked everything else from her mind, even the fact that the only thing he was wearing under the blanket was a pair of boxers.

They had stayed at the scene another hour. The fire had been put out, but no one was allowed back into the building. Residents who didn't have a relative or someone else close by were being sent to a local senior citizens center until other plans could be made. Chad had gotten one of the policemen at the scene to pop the lock on his car. There wasn't much in it, but he did have a gym bag with some spare clothes and sneakers. Chad had managed to pull on a pair of shorts and a T-shirt, but he had wanted to save the sweatpants and sweatshirt for after his shower.

As soon as they entered her house, Chad headed for the phone in the kitchen and stayed on it for a good twenty minutes. She stayed in the living room petting Shamrock, who seemed to be taking this latest commotion in stride.

The sound of Chad's footsteps on the stairs pulled her from the memories.

"Thanks for the loan of the shower. I needed it." Chad stepped into the kitchen.

"No problem." He looked much better. His hair was wet and slicked back and he looked warm and comfortable in the worn sweats. Thick white socks covered his feet. "Did you find everything you needed?" She had pulled out a new toothbrush and the shampoo and soap her brothers used when they visited. None of them liked the flowery smell of hers.

"Yes. Can I use the phone again? I want to call the hospital and check on Mrs. Saleski."

"I figured you would, so I called while you were taking your shower. Mrs. Saleski is fine and resting comfortably. She's being released in the morning. She'll be staying with a niece in the city. As for the other two people who were injured, one was already released from the hospital with a broken arm. The other is in satisfactory condition with a compound fracture of the leg and a broken wrist."

A ghost of a smile touched Chad's mouth for the first time that night. "All that from one phone call?"

"I'm persistent."

"No, you're stubborn." Chad crossed the room and tenderly brushed a wave of her hair behind her ear. "Did I thank you yet for coming to my rescue?"

"I was late." *Late on a lot of things. Late discovering clues in the vision. Late saving your partner's life and late saving two good decent cops from being plowed into by some madman.* "I gather you were the intended victim."

"Definitely. I got that confirmed without your paranormal abilities."

"How?" Tonight in the vision, she'd finally felt the connection between the fire and the other crimes.

"I got a phone call about half a minute before the smoke detectors went off in the hallway."

"From the killer?"

"Yes. When the phone rang, I thought it was you calling, but it wasn't. It was a mechanical voice saying 'Liar, liar, pants on fire. Nose as long as a telephone wire.' Nothing original, but the word *fire* brought me out of bed in hurry."

"The killer warned you? Why? No one else was warned."

"I know. It doesn't make much sense unless the killer misjudged the speed of the fire and was hoping that message would be the last thing I ever heard." Chad pulled her closer as a shudder shook her body. "Or the killer wanted me to escape and lose just about everything I owned."

She buried her face in the crook of his neck. He smelled like soap and fabric softener. "Either way, it sounds like we're dealing with a madman."

"We already knew that, Bridget." His strong arms held her close. "The call I made earlier was to my captain. I told him what happened and about the phone call."

"What did he say?"

"Nothing really, except he wants me down at the station first thing in the morning and that he'd personally contact the arson investigator to see what they found. Maybe we can get a link there, but it's doubtful. But he did agree this sounds like the same man."

It was the same man. There wasn't a doubt in her mind. Chad knew it, too, but he was playing it by the book. She didn't want to think about the fire or the other atrocities. She wanted to think about Chad—think about him spending the night in her house, in her bed.

Chad yawned and dropped a kiss on top of her head.

"It sounds like you're ready for bed."

Chad dropped his arms and stepped back. "A couple hours of sleep will do us both some good." His gaze seemed to land somewhere over her left shoulder. "I'll take the couch."

"You don't have to, Chad." She held her breath and waited. It was the most brazen invitation she had ever offered a man. The thought of almost losing him tonight gave her the courage.

Chad's intense gaze locked on hers for a full minute before lowering to the scar encircling her throat. He slowly shook his head. "I can't."

Bridget closed her eyes as humiliation and pain washed over her. Chad had refused her invitation. She turned and headed out of the kitchen before she made an utter fool out of herself again, this time by crying.

"There's a blanket and pillow in the hall closet. Help yourself to anything else you might need." From the stairs, she called, "Good night, Chad. I'll see you in the morning." She kept moving until she was behind her closed bedroom door.

She kicked off the jeans she'd pulled on over the shorts of her pajamas and climbed into her bed. Her cold and lonely bed.

The past had won. She had seen where Chad's gaze had fallen to, the scar from the electrical cord that had been tightened around her throat. Frank Barelli, Chad's partner, had intended to kill her, to leave no witnesses. Chad had said if he'd been a minute later, she would have died. She disagreed. She wouldn't have given herself thirty more seconds.

She didn't remember too much from that night, which in a way was a blessing. She had taken the prescription sleeping pills a doctor had prescribed for her and had been looking forward to a good night's sleep away from the campus. A guard was posted in the other room. She'd awakened with Barelli already in her room and on top of her. She remembered fighting for all she was worth, which only infuriated Barelli more.

When she had yanked off her attacker's ski mask and discovered who he was, Barelli went into a violent fit and nearly beat her to death before reaching for the lamp on the nightstand. He wrapped the cord around her neck. She had clawed at the wire even after everything went black. The last sound she remembered hearing was shattering wood and Chad's yell of "No!" She never even heard the gunshot that killed Barelli.

The next thing she knew, she was coming to in a hospital. Nearly every inch of her body was black and blue and her face looked like someone had taken a baseball bat to it. Her body had been horribly violated, and the gash around her throat burned like hell. She couldn't talk for nearly five days, but every time a male doctor came into the room to examine her, she cried and cringed with fear.

When she looked in the mirror now, she didn't dwell on the past and its horrors. She concentrated on the strength it had taken her to get over it and the conviction she would never allow something like that to happen to her again. When Chad looked at the scar, he saw the past and the pitiful creature she must have been lying on that bed, naked, bloody, beaten, and gasping for her next breath. Was it any wonder he didn't want her? Who could desire such a pitiful creature?

She pulled the covers up past her shoulders and buried her face deep within the softness of her pillow. No tears formed in her eyes. There weren't any left.

As Bridget left the kitchen, Chad felt like the lowest form of reptile imaginable. He had seen her pain, but it was better for her to suffer a little embarrassment than for him to screw up and get her killed. It had taken every ounce of willpower he possessed to tell her no. He knew what she had been asking, and he had almost said yes—until his gaze encountered the scar encircling her throat.

He had failed her once before. He'd die before he failed her again. Five years ago he had been attracted to Bridget, but there hadn't been any emotional involvement. Now his emotions and every other part of him were involved, including his heart.

Tonight, after coming close to being killed, he could admit the truth to himself. He had fallen in love with Bridget.

He turned off the kitchen light and headed for the living room. The blanket and pillow were where Bridget had told him they would be, but he didn't feel like sleeping. He tossed them onto the couch and carefully placed his revolver on the coffee table, within easy reach. With a weary sigh, he stretched out on the couch and placed his hands behind his head while he stared up at the ceiling. Bridget was up there, all soft and warm and tucked into her big queen-sized brass bed with its old-fashioned quilt.

Her bedroom had surprised him. He had expected something pink or purple with lots of ruffles and bows. Bridget had done the room in blues and white. Lace curtains hung at the windows. The bed did have one of those ruffles on it, but that was it for the feminine frills. Antique oak bureaus and a rocker completed the room, along with thick blue carpeting. It was a room he could feel comfortable in. That not only scared him, it made him smile, which scared him more.

Shamrock jumped up onto the couch and nearly gave him a heart attack. He was reaching for his gun before it dawned on him who or what it was. The cat curled up on top of his feet and promptly fell asleep. Sleeping with Shamrock was a lot safer than sleeping with Bridget.

He glanced over at the front door. From the hall

light, he could see the chain was on. The patio door had been locked when he left the kitchen. Bridget had assured him the windows were all locked. Maybe he should double check them anyway, but there was no reason to suspect Bridget was in any danger. Then again, there had been no reason to suspect some madman would set the entire third floor of his apartment building on fire, either. Shamrock's weight on his feet stopped him from getting up to check the windows.

It didn't matter. He would hear anyone trying to break in. He was too keyed up to sleep. He had a thousand questions running through his mind, but the most important one didn't have anything to do with Mark's murder or the fire tonight. It had to do with Bridget. What the hell was he going to say to her in a few hours when she came back downstairs?

Chad leaned back and glanced out the car window at the passing scenery. It was one of those beautiful, crisp fall mornings, full of sunshine and colorful leaves. He'd appreciate it more if the driver would show some emotion besides politeness. Formal, cool politeness.

Bridget had joined him in her kitchen a little after eight this morning, all dressed and ready for work. Since he was still up pondering the Fates and thinking about Bridget when he heard the shower start, he'd made coffee, eggs, and toast. Bridget had politely eaten her breakfast and complimented him on his cooking skills—as if it would have taken Julia

Child to scramble a few eggs and butter the toast. He'd been living on his own since he was eighteen. He knew how to feed himself. Heck, he even knew how to do his own laundry.

Bridget had been a gracious hostess, but her icy distance was driving him crazy. She had politely and graciously offered him the use of her car, which he accepted because he had no other choice. A locksmith was one of the first people on his list to call. He needed his own car. He also needed clothes, money, a new credit card, and to notify his insurance carrier.

The list seemed endless, and Bridget had offered to help. After the way he'd hurt her last night, he had been surprised by her offer. When he thought about it, he realized that was who Bridget was, a nice decent person. The woman didn't seem to know how to hold a grudge. She still insisted he had never failed her, when anyone with two brain cells to rub together could see he'd failed her big time. Bridget was just too damned nice for her own good.

The strip mall where The Garden of Eden was located came into view. They hadn't said more than two words to each other since they got into her car. He was unsure of what to say or even where to begin. An apology seemed appropriate, but he wasn't sorry. Given the choice of making love with Bridget or possibly saving her life, he'd choose saving her life every time.

Bridget drove the car into the parking lot and parked in front of her shop. "If you need the car past five o'clock, I could get Mary to give me a lift home."

"No, that's okay. I'll have the car back to you by

then, or I'll be here to give you a lift." He got out of the car and joined Bridget on the sidewalk.

She removed two keys from her ring and handed them to him.

"Open up the shop and I'll go through it with you."

"Why?" Bridget glanced at the store in front of her in confusion.

"After last night, I'm a little edgy about everything. Call it paranoia, but since I'm here it will only take two minutes to put my mind at ease."

Bridget unlocked the door and stepped inside. "Well, since it's your mind we're putting at ease."

He glanced at her and wondered what that comment meant. It didn't sound like the same emotionless hostess from this morning. His alert glance took in the large plate glass window of her store, which reflected the parking lot and the busy main road behind him. He started to follow Bridget into the shop when the reflection of a blue Taurus caught his eye. The car pulled over to the side of the road and stopped.

Without turning around, he continued into the store and closed and locked the door behind him. He could feel Bridget's gaze on him as he hid himself in the shadows and stared out across the street. The front fender was dented, and there might be damage to the headlight area. He couldn't be certain from this viewpoint. "Do you have a back door?"

"Yes, it leads to the alley. There's nothing out there but garbage dumpsters." Bridget stepped closer to the front door to see what he was staring at.

"Don't move!"

Bridget froze. "Why?"

"A blue Taurus just stopped across the street. It has fender damage." He made his way to the counter, found a pen and paper, and quickly wrote a number. "I want you to call this number and tell them what I just told you. Give them this address and stay away from the windows. I'm going out the back way and try to come up on the car from a blind side. Lock the back door after I'm out, and don't open up for anyone but me."

Bridget's hand trembled as she took the paper. "Do you think it's the same car?"

"It's possible." He glanced at her pale face. "Everything is going to be okay." He couldn't resist a quick kiss. "I promise." He turned and was halfway through the back office when her voice stopped him.

"Chad?"

"What?" The back door was a nice thick metal one. Besides the lock on the knob, there were two deadbolts. All three were locked.

Bridget appeared in the doorway. "Be careful."

He smiled and winked. "Always." He turned the locks and quietly let himself out.

The smell of garbage assaulted him as he quickly made his way down the deserted alley. His gun was in his hand as he reached the other end and slowly made his way around the side of the building.

The Taurus was still parked where it had been, roughly in the middle of the mall, but on the far side of the main road. He would have to cross the busy road in broad daylight.

He had lied to Bridget. There was no blind side. His best hope was whoever was driving was busy keeping an eye on Bridget's store and not the road. Backup was on its way, but would it get here in time? Whoever was driving that Taurus had killed Mark, run over John and Dan, and then set his apartment building on fire last night. It was one damned busy person, and he couldn't chance waiting for backup.

He ran across the parking lot of a gas station and a fast food restaurant before attempting to cross the main road. He jammed his gun into the waistband of his sweats, waited for an opening in traffic, and then took off running.

The driver of the Taurus spotted him before he cleared the exit signs of the fast food restaurant. Tires squealing, engine floored, the Taurus ate up the asphalt and headed straight up the road.

Chad had made it across both lanes of traffic and was on the side of the road before he glanced at the car. It was driving illegally on his side of the road and approaching at a high rate of speed, headed right at him. The sun's glare obscured any view of who might be driving, but whoever it was meant to kill him.

He raised his gun and fired at the driver. The car swerved dangerously for a moment, then straightened out and kept coming. He didn't have time to fire a second shot. He dived out of the way just in time.

Dirt and mulch from some landscape barrier dug into him, and then the concrete curb stopped his roll. He shook off the pain, jumped to his feet, and ran to the side of the road. His gun was still clutched in his hand, but there were too many other cars to risk getting off another shot. He sat down on the curb that had rudely and abruptly stopped his roll and rubbed his elbow. A ghost of a smile tilted up the corners of his mouth. He had another clue, and with any luck it would help catch the killer. He had managed to read the license plate.

Bridget reached his side before he even heard sirens approaching. So much for backup.

"Chad! Are you hurt?" She sounded rushed and out of breath.

He slowly stood up and refused to groan or rub his right hip. "I'm fine." He put the safety back on the gun and slid it into his waistband. "I thought I told you to stay in the shop."

"No, you told me to stay away from the windows." Bridget was still sucking in air after her recent run.

"Same thing." He moved to stand at the side of the road as sirens filled the air. He waved his arms and drew their attention. The cavalry had arrived.

"Different words."

He stared at her until the approaching police cars drew his attention. Didn't she realize what the killer's showing up at her shop meant? He turned and walked over to the first police car that pulled into the parking lot next to them.

Within five minutes all the cars but one had been dispatched to search for the blue 1990 Taurus with front-end damage and now a bullet hole through the windshield. The one left had given them a ride back to Bridget's shop.

Chad had just gotten off the phone with his captain. While agreeing to send someone over to watch over Bridget and her shop, he still demanded to see Chad's butt downtown immediately, but Chad needed to talk to Bridget first.

Mary, who had been waiting at the shop when they returned, and Bridget were behind the counter discussing business. "Mary, can you handle the store for a few minutes? I need to talk to Bridget in her office."

"Sure." Mary gave him a curious look, but didn't question why a patrol car was still sitting in front of the shop.

He followed Bridget into the office, shut the door, and walked over to the back door and double checked the locks. "Make sure these stay locked at all times."

"The only time I unlock them is when I take the garbage out." Bridget sat down at her desk. "What did you need to talk to me about?"

"You're not going to like it. In a way I can't blame you, so I'm going to give you a choice."

"A choice about what?"

"Your safety." He paced the small room. He had seen closets bigger than Bridget's office. "The killer didn't just show up outside your shop, Bridget. We were followed here this morning, and that means the killer knows where you live. You can't follow someone unless you have a starting point."

"I know." Bridget's fingers trembled as she smoothed her flowing skirt over her knees. "I figured that out myself."

"I'm sorry for dragging you into this."

"You've got that backwards. I dragged you into it. I went to you first, Chad."

"It doesn't matter who did what first. What's important is that the killer knows where you live and work. You could be his next target."

"By the way that car was heading right for you, I'd say *you* were his next target."

He wasn't going to get into technicalities with her. "You can go to live with Dillon or one of your other brothers until we apprehend the killer, or I can set you up in a safe house under protection. Which do you prefer?"

"Neither, Chad. If—and it's a mighty big if—I'm the next intended victim, I will never lead a killer to one of my brothers' families. That isn't an option. As for a safe house . . ." Bridget gave him a look that clearly stated her opinions on police guards and safe houses. "After what happened before, do you honestly believe I would willingly go into another safe house? Who's to say this killer isn't a cop, too?"

A shudder ripped through him. Lord, what if she was right? What if the killer was hiding right under his nose again? He could see her reasoning for not running to one of her brothers. Reading was close enough to Philadelphia that the killer could follow her. He surely couldn't blame her for not trusting a safe house and a guard after what happened before.

"That only leaves one alternative, Bridget."

"Which is?"

"You're getting a new roommate."

"Who might that be?"

"Me." He placed both hands on her desk and leaned forward. "I'll be living with you, working with you, and breathing down your neck twenty-four hours a day. You will go nowhere without me, and I'll be there every time you turn around. I'll be underfoot and in your hair."

He locked gazes with her and issued his last warning. "If you ever deliver another invitation like you did last night, I'll take you up on the offer. Last night I used up all my willpower, Bridget. I want you too much to refuse you twice. So think long and hard before you decide."

He couldn't tell by her eyes if he'd just shocked her or not. "What do you have to say to that?"

Bridget calmly raised one eyebrow and said, "There's a spare key to my house under the pot of chrysanthemums on the second step."

He turned and, without a word, stormed out of her office. He'd wanted her to pick one of the other options so she'd be out of harm's way and he wouldn't be responsible for her. He couldn't fail her again. So why the hell had his stomach just bottomed out and every ounce of spare blood he possessed just rushed to one obvious place? And why was his heart doing flip-flops faster than Fred Astaire could tap dance?

Bridget stood under the shower longer than necessary and allowed the hot water to ease away her tension. Chad had used the shower first, and the scent of his soap and shampoo was still in the air. She loved that scent. For the past two nights, it had given her a secret pleasure just to smell it in her bathroom. Chad had been true to his word. He was now her roommate and constant guard, even though he needed the guard more than she did.

They knew who the killer was and even understood the killer's twisted logic. Problem was, they didn't know *where* the killer was.

The license plate had led them directly to Nancy Barelli, Frank's sister. They found the abandoned Taurus near the apartment where she'd been living. There were no signs of Nancy, and Chad's bullet had missed. The police had dug it out of the seat, and there wasn't a trace of blood anywhere to be found. The thirty-eight revolver that had been used to kill Mark Monterey had been found empty and shoved under the front seat.

After Frank's death and the subsequent announcement he had been the rapist, Nancy had suffered a nervous breakdown and had been committed. Most of her records were sealed, but considering the charges against her, especially the murder of a police officer, they had been able to find out some background information. Nancy and Frank had lived together since their parents' death when Nancy had been eighteen and Frank twenty-four. They were brother and sister, but they were also lovers. Nancy's anger was directed more at the thought that Frank had been cheating on her with the coeds than at his actual death.

With another wave of state cutbacks to mental institutions, the institution's doctors decided after five years of treatment, Nancy Barelli was well enough to be released back into society under a social worker's supervision. The overworked and underpaid social worker had reported Nancy Barelli missing four weeks ago when she didn't show up for her scheduled appointment and couldn't be reached at her apartment. The timing was perfect.

The police believed Nancy was out for revenge against Chad for killing her brother. First she killed Chad's partner, then tried to kill two of his friends by running them down. Next she set his apartment building on fire, either to kill him or to destroy everything he owned.

Chad believed Nancy would go after Bridget next. Bridget wasn't too sure. Nancy was getting desperate and sloppy. Nancy had lost her car and probably by now knew they were looking for her. The smart money would be on Nancy's trying to finish the job and take Chad out.

Bridget shivered under the hot water and quickly turned it off. She didn't want to think about anything happening to Chad.

She stepped out of the shower and wrapped a towel around her wet hair and another around her quivering body. Chad was safe. He was downstairs camped out on her couch, as he had been the past three nights. She hadn't reissued the invitation to him to share her bed for fear of being rejected once again. He'd said he wouldn't turn her offer down, but she hadn't seen any signs he would accept it, either.

Chad had been a perfect gentlemen since moving in and laying siege to her home and to her shop, even though he gave orders like a five-star general. He had to have taken caution lessons from the Secret Service. In short, he was driving her nuts. Most disturbing of all, he hadn't kissed her once.

Bridget finished drying off, put on her pajamas, and headed for bed. Her good nights to Chad had been said a while ago. She climbed into bed and frowned at the empty spot at her feet. Shamrock had deserted her to sleep with Chad. She couldn't fault the cat. Given a choice, she'd sleep with Chad, too.

Sleep came slowly, but deeply, within an hour.

Bridget knew she was dreaming and smiled in her sleep. She and Chad were in her backyard raking up leaves one minute and rolling around in them the next. Chad laughed as she pinned him to the ground and tickled him. Lord, how she loved that rare laugh. Shamrock joined the wrestling match for a moment before pouncing off to chase after some bug. With crackling leaves under them, around them, and still slowly falling from the tree above them, Chad kissed her.

It was the perfect dream, and Bridget allowed herself to sink farther into it. Chad's kiss became hungrier and she met that hunger with an urgency of her own.

The edges of the dream started to blur and fade, but she ignored that and concentrated on Chad's kisses. The leaves were replaced by squares. She pushed the squares away and frowned as Chad started to dissolve beneath her. She reached desperately for him, but could only grab mist that slipped through her fingers. The squares grew until they covered the backyard and beyond.

Green and white squares, like a checkerboard. A glass vase crashed down, bringing with it water and daisies, dozens of white and yellow daisies.

It wasn't a checkerboard. It was her shop. The Garden of Eden had a green and white checkered tile floor.

Bridget frowned at the vision. What did it mean? She was still frowning and concentrating when from the far corner a smudge appeared, a tiny smudge that expanded and flowed toward the vase and the spilled water and flowers.

She stared in horror as the smudge became clearer and more distinct in color. Deep crimson red flowed across the tile floor to mix with the water and turn it a lighter shade of red. Blood! She was seeing blood, lots of it, flowing across her shop floor!

A scream ripped from her throat as she struggled for consciousness. She didn't want to see more, but she couldn't lose the vision. The blood kept coming and she kept screaming.

"Bridget! Wake up, Bridget." Chad pulled her up and was gently shaking her. "Come on, honey, open your eyes."

She felt his hands and heard his voice, but she kept seeing the blood. Too much blood. No one could live and lose that much blood, could they?

"Bridget, you're scaring me! Wake up, come on." Chad's hands shook her a little harder. "Please, honey, let it go!"

The tile floor and its gruesome portrait of the future vanished and she slowly opened her eyes. The first thing she saw was Chad's pale, concerned face. She managed a shaky, "Sorry."

Chad sat on the side of the bed and pulled her into his arms and held her tight. "You were screaming."

She pressed her heated face against his bare chest and breathed in the scent of his soap. "It was a nightmare."

"A nightmare or a vision?"

She kept her face buried beneath his chin so he couldn't see the lie in her eyes. Her brothers always told her she was a terrible liar. "Nightmare." She shuddered and his strong arms closed in tighter. Lord, how safe she felt in this man's arms.

"It must have been a bad one." Chad sounded unsure whether he believed her or not. "Want to talk about it?"

"No." She shook her head violently. If she told Chad what she had just seen, he would never let her set foot into her shop again.

Her hands caressed his warm back from the top of his shoulders to the waistband of his new jeans. Either he'd yanked them on before rushing upstairs, or he had been sleeping in them. She felt the quickening of his heartbeat and the unsteadiness of his breathing. Chad wasn't as unaffected by her closeness as he wanted her to believe.

What if that had been her blood she had seen? What if she was the one to die next and Chad couldn't save her? Did she want to die without experiencing what making love with Chad would be like, without making love with the man she loved?

Before she could think things through or worry about another rejection, she blurted out, "I know you don't think I'm attractive after the way you found me when Barelli was done and all. But could you stay and make love with me tonight?"

TEN

"Where the hell did you get an insane idea like that?" Chad pushed her back by her shoulders and stared down at her face.

He couldn't believe he'd heard her right. Bridget thought he wasn't attracted to her because of what happened with Barelli. Was she out of her mind?

Bridget tried to duck her head, but he wouldn't let her. "From you," came her shy response.

"From me? When have I ever said or indicated any such thing?" He knew he wasn't what some would call a ladies' man, but he wasn't some insensitive jerk, either.

After the horrors she had suffered and the way she confronted life head on and refused to allow Barelli to continue to make a victim out of her, he had the deepest admiration for her. Bridget was one of the most courageous women he'd ever met. Her inner strength was equal to that of ten good tough city cops. Half the time he was in awe of her. The other half was pure lust.

Bridget lowered her hands to her lap and gazed at the wall over his shoulder. "Every time we start to get . . . intimate, you take one look at the scar around my throat and back off as if it would burn you." Her trembling fingers reached up and touched the thin line of damaged flesh. "You see me as I was that night and you can't get away from me fast enough."

His heart felt as if it was being torn from his body. He had done this to her. He had been the one to make her doubt her own desirability, not Barelli. With fingers that shook and a silent prayer for the words to make her understand, he gently cupped her cheeks and made her look at him. "There could be another reason the sight of this mark"—his thumbs lowered and he softly caressed the scar—"would make me stop and back away."

"What reason?" Bridget's soft green eyes glowed with something he would like to think was hope.

"Guilt."

"Guilt? Whose guilt?"

"Mine." He slid his palms down her cheeks and pressed them against the satiny smoothness of her throat. Her heart beat wildly beneath his hands. "I should have stopped him sooner." He lowered his head and placed a gentle kiss upon the thin white line. "Because of me, you bear this mark, this constant reminder of what Barelli did."

Bridget tilted her head back as his lips touched her throat. "No, you're wrong, Chad. It wasn't your fault." A soft sigh escaped her mouth.

"I should have figured it out sooner." He nipped at the pulse thundering in the side of her neck, and then his tongue gently caressed the spot. "Barelli never should have gotten near you." He pulled her closer as visions of the past flooded his mind—Bridget broken and bleeding, spread out under Barelli, Bridget fighting for her life; Bridget clawing at the cord, fighting for her next breath that almost never came.

A violent shudder shook his body. "I'd kill him again if I could."

"You're doing it again." Bridget's hands pushed against his shoulders. "You're not seeing me, Chad. You're seeing the past."

The pain and frustration that threaded through her shaky voice pulled him back to the present. He gazed into her eyes and marveled at the emotions swirling in their depths—eyes that could see the future while combating the horrors of the past. Eyes that knew and saw too much.

"You're right, Bridget. I was seeing the past, but it doesn't change how I feel for you." He reached out and slowly traced her lush lower lip. "I want you so badly that I've been aching for weeks and going out of my mind."

She moistened her parted lips with the tip of her tongue. "I've been aching, too, Chad."

He closed his eyes and groaned. "Do you have any idea what that mouth of yours does to me?"

A fleeting smile played at the corner of her lips. "It isn't doing anything to you right now."

He chuckled at the teasing light that sparkled in her eyes. He had walked right into that one. "I want more than your mouth, Bridget. I want all of you, every lovely silky smooth inch of you. I want to touch you, to taste you."

His hands spanned her waist and slowly moved upward. The soft cotton of the T-shirt she had worn to bed bunched beneath his fingers. "I want you under me with your legs wrapped tight around my waist. I want to be buried so deep inside you I'll need a map to find my way back out." His hands cupped her breasts and the mere weight of them caused his fingers to quiver. "I want so damned much from you it scares me at times."

Bridget arched her back and pressed more fully into his hands. Her jutting nipples pushed into his palms. "You're not the only one who's scared, Chad."

He moved his thumbs over the cotton-covered protruding nubs and watched in fascination as they hardened more. His mouth went dry and his jeans became uncomfortably tight. He raised his gaze to hers. Something in her voice caused him to frown. He didn't think she was referring to her feelings toward him. "What scares you?"

Bridget glanced down at his hands, the bulge in his jeans, and the bed beneath them. "This."

He slowly lowered his hands and studied her face. "My touching you scares you?"

"No, it makes me want more, and that's the problem." Bridget wouldn't meet his gaze, and a tide of pink climbed high into her cheeks. It was a first. He'd never seen her blush before.

"Is it the 'more' that's upsetting you?" Maybe she was scared he was going to stop again. He wasn't stopping tonight. He couldn't. He pressed his

thumbs under her chin and forced her head up. He
wanted to be able to see her face.

Bridget nodded and shifted her gaze to somewhere over his shoulder. The becoming pink blush
turned red, and she worried her lower lip with her
teeth.

"Out with it, Bridget." Seeing those teeth sink into
that sinfully lush lip was pushing him to the edge.
In a minute he was going to lose his precarious grip
on what was left of his self-control.

"It's been a long time, that's all." A sigh of relief
punctuated her remark. It was as if she had just con-
fessed a deep secret, one she'd been afraid to share
with him.

The hair on the back of his neck bristled. It was
the same physical reaction he got during an inter-
view with a suspect when he stumbled across something very important to a case. "Exactly how long
has it been?"

Soft green eyes locked with his own intense stare.
When Bridget's answer came, it was so soft he could
hardly hear it. "Five years."

He flinched and closed his eyes, but he didn't
lower his hands. Five years! Bridget hadn't been with
a man since Barelli had violated her. His fingers
trembled against her chin and he wanted to run like
hell.

He slowly opened his eyes and studied the silent
plea in hers. "I'm a little confused, Bridget. You told
me you got on with your life and even dated."

"Dating and sleeping with someone aren't the
same thing, Chad. There's a world of difference."

"I know." He knew the difference, but it seemed the world they were living in didn't. He had just swept Bridget with the world's moral brush and the strokes didn't match. "Why haven't you had a deeper relationship with a man? You're an attractive, intelligent, and desirable woman. Are the men blind as well as stupid in this part of the city?"

Bridget shrugged. "Mr. Right never walked into The Garden of Eden and demanded to see Eve."

His eyes narrowed as they tried to read her face. Bridget was hiding something. The hair on the back of his neck was still standing on end. He slowly shook his head. "Try another one."

"All right. You want to know the truth?" Bridget pulled away from his hands and backed up until she was leaning against a stack of pillows and the brass headboard. She wrapped her arms around her knees and glared at him.

"The truth never hurt anyone."

"Men scared me." Bridget shook her head. "No, that's not right. Men terrified me." Defiance burned like green fire in her eyes. "I was terrified of their height, their strength, their entire physical presence."

She puckered her lips and blew a wayward lock of hair away from her face with a weary sigh. "When I couldn't find a man who appealed to me, I started to panic. I knew something was wrong with me, so I forced myself to go out on dates with men who held not one spark of interest for me. They were nice, decent men with good jobs and interesting lives. My mother, my grandmother, my father, and every one of my brothers would have approved of any one of them."

Huge tears pooled in her eyes. "I forced myself to stand there and accept their good night kisses while my mind screamed in terror and my body remembered everything Barelli had done to it."

He leaned forward and captured a tear as it spilled over and ran down her cheek. "You're speaking in the past tense. When did your fear of men change?" He didn't blame her for her fear of men. It would be normal after what she went through. What surprised him was he'd never noticed that fear. Bridget never shied away from his touch, and her response to his kisses was anything but what she had just described.

"The night I came to your apartment. I woke up screaming in your bed and you held me. For the first time in five years, I felt safe in the embrace of a man who wasn't a relative." She brushed at her tears and gave him a small smile. "The way you held me should have sent me into a near panic attack, considering we were sitting on your bed. It didn't."

He glanced down at her blue checked cotton sheets and the hand-stitched quilt. "We're sitting on a bed now, only this time it's yours. Are you afraid now?"

She shook her head.

"What are you feeling, then?" The last thing he wanted was for Bridget to be afraid of him or of the physical act of making love.

She swiped at the last of her tears. "Stupid."

"Stupid?" He hadn't expected that answer. "Why
re you feeling stupid?"

"I've dreamed about getting you in my bed for
quite some time now." She pressed her cheek to her
knee and gave him a funny little look. "In all those
dreams, not once was I crying."

"Were you ever afraid in any of those dreams?"
His body was hard and throbbing. Bridget had
dreamed of making love with him. If her dreams
were half as erotic as his and she wasn't panicking,
there was one hell of a good chance he wasn't leaving
his bed till morning.

"I've never been afraid of you, Chad, in or out of
my dreams. Afraid *for* you, yes. *Of* you, never."

"Would you tell me if you were?"

"Yes."

He believed her. Bridget was a terrible liar. That
was why he didn't believe a nightmare had caused
that terror-filled scream earlier when he'd raced up
the stairs and lost five years off his life before he
even reached her room. She obviously didn't want
to discuss the vision tonight, which was fine with him.
It could wait till morning. He had more important
things on his mind.

He stretched out across the middle of the bed and
danced his fingers across the tops of her feet. He
smiled when her toes curled under.

"So in these dreams of yours, I gather we weren't
sleeping?"

Bridget shook her head as a splash of pink bright-
ened her cheeks.

He turned on his side and propped his head up

with one hand. With his other hand, he pulled one of Bridget's legs toward him and started to caress the limb from the tip of her toes to mid thigh. "Were we any good together?"

Bridget seemed to have a hard time finding her voice. "Very."

His hand gently cupped the ankle of her other foot and pulled it toward him. "When we were . . finished, how did you feel?"

He could tell by the flush staining her cheeks and the berry hard nipples pressing against her T-shirt that Bridget was responding to his touch and the added stimulation of her dreams. He wanted her more than willing and ready. He wanted her to be the aggressor. She had to be the one in control this first time.

Bridget tilted her head as she pressed the soles of her feet against his chest. "Whole."

His hand stopped an inch shy of the hem of the boxer shorts she was wearing. He cocked one eyebrow. "Whole?"

She wiggled her toes against his chest and playfully tugged at the hair covering it. "Satisfied, content, exhausted." She gave him such a beguiling smile he felt his own toes curl. "You know, Chad, whole."

"That's a lot to ask from one man." The satisfied, content, and exhausted part he thought he could handle. The *whole* part worried him. He wanted the first time with Bridget to be perfect. She deserved it perfect. So how did one make a woman whole?

Her delicate foot rubbed down his chest, but stopped at the waistband of his jeans. Half an instep nore and she would be pressing against the bulge threatening to split his jeans in two.

A century ago, mules hadn't been able to pull these jeans apart, but he had a feeling tonight would be the ultimate test of durability.

Her big toe teased the brass button. "I think you might be up to the challenge."

He gripped her ankle and brought her foot back up to rest against his chest. "There's only two rules tonight, Bridget."

"Rules?"

"First, the light stays on."

He wasn't going to let her hide in the dark. He wanted to be able to read her every expression. At the first sight of her being afraid, he was calling a halt, no matter how far along they were or how much physical discomfort to himself he might cause. Having Bridget afraid wasn't an option.

Her white even teeth worried her lip for a moment before she nodded.

"Rule two, you're in control. We're going to go at your pace. When you want something, you're going to have to ask. Say stop and we stop."

Bridget shook her head and tried to pull her feet away from his chest. He held them there. "Chad, I don't have a pace."

"Yes, you do." He lifted one delicate foot and lightly kissed the inside of her ankle. "All you have to do is find it."

Bridget shivered and closed her eyes as heat spiked up her leg. She had to find her pace and take control of their lovemaking, all with a hundred-watt lightbulb spotlighting her every move. Duplicating Ein stein's Theory of Relativity would be easier. "I don' know where to start."

Chad picked up her other foot and repeated th kiss. "Where do you want to start?"

"Kissing." His kisses made her lose every inhibi tion she ever possessed. "I want to kiss you."

"So kiss me." Chad reclined across the middle o her bed, waiting for her. His sleepy-eyed star seemed to be hiding something. She had to wonde what it was.

She pushed off the headboard and stretched ou next to him close enough to feel the heat of his body but not close enough to be touching. Her finger reached out to caress his jaw, only to halt in midair "What if I do something wrong?"

Chad smiled and pulled on her hand until it reste against his cheek. "There is no wrong in this Bridget. There's only right."

Her fingernail lightly scraped at the shadowy bris tles covering his jaw.

"I should have shaved." He closed his hand around hers and pulled her fingers to his lips.

His teasing bites at her fingers caused her to shive with delight and press closer. The tips of her breast swayed against his chest with every breath she took.

"No." She leaned closer and pressed a quick ligh kiss to the corner of his mouth. "I like it."

Her mouth returned to his, and this time her lips played and nibbled. The tip of her tongue followed the seam of his mouth until he opened and allowed her entrance.

She wrapped her arms around him and pulled him closer to deepen the kiss. Their tongues danced and heat swirled around her, drawing her in deeper, making her want. Making her burn. His skin beneath her palms felt like warm silk.

She stroked his back, and rock-hard muscles quivered under her fingers. Heat spiked and arced between them, and still it wasn't enough. She needed to touch all of him. She needed his touch. His strong fingers were caressing her back, but it wasn't enough. It wasn't nearly enough. She wanted it all.

Desire pulsed deep within her as she broke the kiss and lightly bit his shoulder. With fingers that trembled, she grabbed hold of the hem of her shirt and yanked it over her head in one fluid motion. It landed somewhere over the side of the bed. She glanced at the gold flecks of hunger burning in Chad's eyes and issued a one-word plea. "More."

Chad slowly skimmed his hand across the peaks of her breasts as his mouth slanted down onto hers. She sighed with pleasure and then gasped with need as he rolled her nipple between his fingers. Liquid heat pooled between her thighs, and she arched her hips against the front of his jeans. The hard column of his arousal pressed against her. The strokes of his tongue matched a rhythm her body knew and understood.

She pulled her mouth away from the heat of his and arched her throat. A soft whisper for more tore from her mouth.

Chad groaned something primitive and wild as his mouth blazed a trail of wet kisses down her throat to the peak of her straining nipples. She nearly shattered into a million pieces as his teeth nipped and his lips tugged at the sensitive bud. Chad's warm, large hands cupped her bottom and pressed her hips more fully against him. She needed to get closer.

Her breath came in ragged gasps as she shoved the cotton boxers she had worn to bed over her hips and down her thighs. Her legs kicked them the rest of the way off as she reached for the snap of Chad's jeans.

Chad's strong fingers grabbed hold of her hands and brought them to his lips. His voice was uneven and harsh. "No."

Her gaze shot to his. "No?" Hunger burned in his eyes so bright and fierce she was afraid it might consume him—consume them both. Chad couldn't possibly be stopping now.

"I'm not stopping, Bridget." Chad kissed the tip of one of her fingers and gently sucked it into his mouth. His tongue swirled around it before releasing it. A guilty smile teased the corner of his mouth. "It's just that if you touch me now, it will be all over."

Her gaze lowered to the bulge in his jeans and she bit her lower lip to hide the smile threatening to break across her face. "Oh."

Chad released her hands and unsnapped his own jeans. In one graceful motion, he stood up and removed the final barrier between them. Chad pulled a foil-wrapped condom from his back pocket and tossed it onto the bed before dropping his jeans and underwear to the floor.

She watched in awe as Chad's natural form and

beauty revealed itself. He stood perfectly still and allowed her gaze to travel the length of his body. He was magnificent, and not even a shadow of fear crossed her mind. Her gaze slid to the silver-wrapped packet on the bed. "Are you always prepared?"

Chad released the breath he had been holding and stretched out again across the bed. "No." His warm fingers stroked the curve of her hip. "I warned you that if you invited, I was accepting." They both lay on their sides, facing each other, seeing each other.

Her fingers trailed through the soft curls across his chest and grazed the rigid muscles of his abdomen. He shuddered beneath her touch and she grew bolder, but stopped her teasing when Chad's hand slid up the inside of her thigh. She forgot to breathe when he bent his head and pulled one of her nipples deep within his mouth.

His warm fingers climbed higher, and she instinctively bent her leg. His touch was light and gentle as he threaded his way through the curls between her thighs and touched her where she ached to be touched.

She arched against his fingers and sighed when he slipped one inside her.

Chad groaned and released the nub. "God, Bridget, you're so hot and wet." A second finger joined the first and she jerked her hips with wild pleasure. This was what she wanted.

She pressed against his hand, closed her eyes against the pleasure, and breathlessly pleaded, "More."

Chad left her to reach behind him for the foil package. She moaned with frustration.

"Shhhh . . . I'm coming." Chad prepared himself and then lifted one of her legs over his hip.

"No"—she buried her face against his neck—"not without me."

Chad's chuckle was choppy as he slowly entered her. "No, my love"—his warm hands pressed her closer—"not without you."

He filled her and she bit his neck as intense rapture coiled deep and tight. He started to pull out and she locked her leg around his hip.

Chad flexed his hips and filled her deeper than before. She purred with pleasure and he captured the sound with his mouth. She brought her leg higher and felt him plunge in deeper. She had never made love while lying on her side before, and she knew why Chad hadn't taken the dominant position above her. She loved him more for it, but it wasn't necessary. She could never compare this feeling with what had happened in the past.

When Chad thrust again, she met him halfway and whispered, "Again."

Chad playfully bit her lip. "Demanding, aren't you?"

She contracted the walls surrounding his arousal and heard him groan with pleasure. "Rule number two."

She smiled as his thrusts became faster and deeper.

Her smile quickly faded as the coil inside her tightened to an unbearable pressure. With every thrust it tightened farther. Her hips met his with increasing force and her lungs seemed not to get enough air. "Chad . . . please."

He worked his blunt-tipped fingers between their straining bodies to touch her gently where their bodies merged. The coil shattered, taking her with it. A cry of release broke from her lips and Chad's quickly followed.

Bridget burrowed deeper under the quilt and into Chad's embrace. He had been the one to turn out the light and move them under the blankets. She had glimpsed his revolver within easy reach on the table next to the bed before he'd turned out the light.

She wrapped an arm around his waist and placed her head upon his shoulder. She felt safe and content. More important, she felt whole.

Chad had given her that feeling. Was it any wonder she had fallen in love with him? Her guard, her protector, and now her lover.

He kissed her forehead and then gently squeezed her closer and whispered, "Still awake?"

"Hmmm . . . you're warm." She loved the feel of skin against skin. She moved her leg over one of his.

His fingers tenderly combed through her hair. "How do you feel?"

She placed a kiss against his chest, snuggled closer, and yawned. "Whole. I feel whole."

His fingers stilled for a moment before they continued their tender stroking. "Good, I'm glad." Another kiss, this one landing on the top of her head. "Get some sleep now. I'm here."

The fuzzy world of sleep and dreams was pulling

her under when it crossed her mind she hadn't told Chad she loved him. She'd tell him tomorrow, that's what she'd do. A smile graced her mouth as sleep finally claimed her.

Bridget jammed another delicate pink rosebud into the arrangement she was working on. To be more accurate, the one she was trying to work on. Chad's questions kept interfering with her work.

"I'm telling you for the last time, Chad, it wasn't a vision. It was a nightmare. A plain, ordinary nightmare." She reached for another rosebud and refused to look at him.

Chad leaned against the counter and watched her every move. "You're lying."

"I am not." She glanced at the clock on the wall and wondered for the tenth time in twenty minutes when Mary would get back from her lunch break. Chad couldn't question her with Mary buzzing around the shop, so he had waited until her full-time employee took her break. He was playing dirty pool, but she knew she deserved it after the trick she had pulled on him this morning.

She had awakened to a cup of freshly poured coffee and her robe. She had slipped into her robe and had barely tasted the coffee before his questions started.

Chad had known her screams from the night before weren't caused by a bad dream and that the visions had returned.

She hadn't wanted to admit it or discuss it, so she

undid the sash on her robe and shrugged out of the garment. Very softly, she told Chad she was taking her shower and he was invited to join her.

Chad had joined her, and they never made it out of the shower until all the hot water was used up. She'd had to rinse the last of the soap out of her hair with cold water, but she hadn't cared.

They'd had to grab breakfast on the run, or they never would have made it to the shop on time. As it was, Mary had pulled into the parking lot right behind them.

"If you're not lying, why can't you look at me?" Chad's arms were folded across his chest. She could see the holster and gun under his sports coat.

"Because you're getting me mad, and I don't want to look at you when I'm mad." She pricked her finger on a thorn and glared at him, as if it had been his fault. "See what you made me do?" She thrust her finger into her mouth and sucked at the drop of blood the small prick had caused.

"Me? You're the one who's jamming them in there like . . ." Chad's voice trailed off as a customer stepped into the shop. His eyes immediately cut to the woman and the two small children she had dragged in with her.

Bridget smiled at the harried-looking woman. She had seen a picture of Nancy Barelli. Unless she was a Hollywood makeup artist who had the ability to take roughly five inches off her height and add thirty pounds, this wasn't Nancy. "May I help you?"

"Please." The woman had a desperate edge about her. "I need a centerpiece for a dinner table." One of the boys headed for a display shelf crowded with glass and porcelain objects. The woman grabbed the back of his jacket before he took two steps. "My husband just invited his boss home for dinner tonight." The woman's anxious glance shot to the clock and she groaned.

"Okay. What color is the dining room, kitchen, or wherever the table is?"

"Pinks and burgundies."

"Do you want it to coordinate with the room, or do you want something seasonal?" Her mind raced through her current inventory. Bridget prided herself on knowing exactly what she had on hand at any given time.

"I don't know. What do you suggest?" The woman looked on the verge of tears. She bent and picked up the fussy toddler clinging to her leg and jostled him on her hip.

"Stick to the pinks and burgundies. Oranges and rust would only clash." Bridget searched under the counter and came up with a plastic oblong container. "May I also suggest a couple of long taper candles in it? When lit, they look lovely and classy. More important, the low lighting will conceal a multitude of faults—the meal, the china and linens that have seen better days, or the dusty chandelier."

Bridget pushed the arrangement she had been working on to the side and started to yank containers holding ferns, greens, and flowers out of the refrigerator unit.

"Yes, candles, please." The woman managed a small, grateful smile.

Both boys watched Bridget as her fingers flew and the arrangement materialized before their eyes. Within minutes, she added the finishing touch of three pale pink tapered candles. "Well, what do you think?" A happy customer was one who returned.

"Lovely, simply lovely." The woman pulled out a credit card. "Thank you so much."

"No problem." Bridget rang up the sale and handed each of the boys a lollipop she kept for her youngest customers. "One more suggestion."

"What?" The woman unwrapped the pop for the youngest one still perched on her hip.

"Issac's. It's on Roosevelt Boulevard next to Hoss's car dealership. They have the best selection of already prepared food, and their desserts are out of this world."

She lowered her voice as if she were giving away a state secret. "I'm talking gourmet meals that will melt in your mouth and no one would guess they came from some shop and not your oven."

The woman lost the desperation that had been clinging to her when she entered the shop. "Thanks."

Bridget smiled as she watched the trio pile into a minivan. She turned to Chad, who had perched himself on the stool at the far end of the counter and had watched the whole scene unfold without a word. "My money says she'll pull it off."

Smiling, she started to clean up the mess scattered across the counter.

"I won't bet against that." Chad came up behind

her and wrapped his arms around her waist and nuzzled her neck. "You love what you do, don't you?"

"If I didn't, I wouldn't be here." Her gaze lowered to the green and white tiled floor of her shop. A flash of the vision crossed her sight. Trampled daisies, broken glass, and blood. Lots and lots of blood. She shivered and Chad's arms tightened around her.

"What's wrong?"

"Nothing."

"Stop lying to me, Bridget." Strong gentle hands rubbed at the goosebumps on her arms. "Tell me."

"It's nothing, Chad." She shook her head and the floor was once again just a tiled floor. "Someone must have walked across my grave."

Chad turned her around and shook her by the shoulders. "Don't ever say that!"

Bridget blinked in surprise. She hadn't realized what she'd said until Chad reacted to it. She reached up and smoothed away his scowl with her fingertips. "It's nothing but an old wives' saying, Chad. You say it when you get goosebumps or a sudden chill."

Chad pulled her into his embrace and hugged her close. "Don't say it again. I don't like the sound of it."

She hugged him back and his gun dug into her upper arm, a constant reminder of the danger they were in. "I won't use it again." She pressed a kiss along the side of his neck. "It doesn't mean anything, Chad."

Her gaze fell to the green and white tiled floor beneath them. *Or did it?*

ELEVEN

A terror-filled scream yanked Chad from the black oblivion of sleep. He reached for Bridget and was assaulted by flailing arms and thrashing feet. Her scream seemed endless and came directly from her soul.

"Bridget! Wake up!" He grabbed for her hands and managed to capture one of them. He threw one of his legs over hers and grunted as her free hand connected with his jaw. The strength in those delicate limbs amazed him.

"Come on, Bridget. Open your eyes." He blocked her next swing and shook her shoulder. "Wake up!"

"Noooo . . ." A thin sheen of perspiration coated her skin, and her hand slipped out of his grasp. Bridget pushed desperately at him or at something only she could see.

In the pale light penetrating the room from the hallway, he could see the fear contorting her features. His heart squeezed in agony. He was failing Bridget again. He couldn't make the visions go away. No matter how much she was denying it, he knew this wasn't an ordinary nightmare. The visions had returned, and she wouldn't tell him what they were.

"Come on, love, wake up." He grabbed at her hands and this time succeeded. He anchored them above her head with one hand. "Let it go, Bridget. Let it go!" Three nights he had loved her. Three nights the vision had come.

He cupped her jaw and forced her head to stop its frantic shaking back and forth. The thought of using physical strength to hold her down sickened him. He could never use force against her, but he couldn't sit back and watch her suffer through the visions. Hearing about them was one thing, but seeing what she went through during one was heart wrenching.

"Open your eyes, Bridget. Come on, it's me, Chad." He placed a quick kiss on her eyelids. "Come on, love, let me see those beautiful Irish eyes."

Bridget's feverish fight slowed and then halted completely. He released her arms and lifted his leg off her thighs. A moment later, her eyes slowly opened and he glimpsed the fear and terror that had held her under its spell. He shuddered and pulled her into his arms. God, how much more could one woman endure?

Warm tears splashed against his chest. Each one felt like a shard of glass piercing his heart. He held her and let her cry as his heart bled.

When the storm finally subsided, Bridget pushed away from him and reached for a handful of tissues on the nightstand. A moment later she was back in his arms. Her voice was weak and watery. "Sorry about that."

He reached down, cupped her chin, and forced her to look at him. "Never apologize for something you can't control. It isn't your fault." Moisture still shone in her eyes, but she appeared to have her composure back. "Now will you tell me what you saw?"

"No." Bridget jerked her chin out of his grip and planted a kiss directly above his heart. "Hold me, Chad."

His arms tightened around her trembling body. "At least tell me what you were trying to push back." Thankfully she wasn't giving him the lie about its only being a nightmare. He didn't think he could handle it tonight.

Bridget closed her eyes and shuddered. "It was blood, Chad." Trembling fingers gripped his arms hard enough to leave impressions. "I was trying to hold back a river of blood." Her voice slowly faded as she pressed her face against his chest. "So much blood. So very, very much."

God, and he'd thought the lie was alarming. It was nothing compared to the truth. *A river of blood!* Whose blood? Where? A thousand questions crowded his mind. "Bridget . . ."

"Not now. Please, Chad. Not now."

Her mouth was warm and enticing as it slanted across his in a kiss hot enough to rekindle the desire he thought they had burned out an hour ago. Her full breasts rubbed against his chest and her delicate fingers seduced his senses.

Before he could break the kiss, desire, hot and

heavy, throbbed between his legs. He knew what she was doing and was powerless to stop her. "Bridget, please . . ."

"Tomorrow, Chad." She nipped his lower lip and followed it with slow seductive strokes of her tongue. "I promise tomorrow I'll tell you." Her hot fingers closed around his arousal. "Make love with me, Chad." Her warm kisses covered his chest and slowly made their way lower. "Tonight, make me forget."

Her tongue, warm and moist, playfully circled his navel and he nearly died from the pleasure. His heart slammed against his ribs as her tongue trailed lower, and he knew he was lost. Tomorrow he would have his answers. Tonight he had to love Bridget.

Bridget glanced over at Chad, who was driving. "I'm telling you, men like to receive flowers, too." They were on their way to visit Dan in the hospital and she had insisted on stopping at the shop to pick up an arrangement. It was bad enough Chad had talked her into visiting a complete stranger in the hospital, but she refused to go empty handed.

"Dan's not like most men." Chad rolled his eyes, but continued driving in the direction of her shop, even though he was taking a different route than yesterday and he kept glancing in the rearview mirror to see if they were being followed.

"What do you think he'd like? A couple of girly magazines and a six pack of beer?"

Chad grinned. "In his condition, nix the magazines, but make it a case of cold ones."

"I guess I could make up a bouquet of balloons. We have balloons and a helium tank at the shop."

John had been released from the hospital over a week ago, but two days ago Dan had just undergone his second operation on his hip and leg. She could tell Chad had wanted to visit his friend, so she hadn't put up too much of an argument, even though meeting someone for the first time while he was flat on his back in pain and dressed in a hospital gown wasn't a good way to make an acquaintance.

"No balloons. Last time I visited Dan, his room looked like a carnival scene."

"Then flowers it is." She reached over and held one of his hands. "I promise to make it as manly as possible."

"You do that."

Bridget smiled and relaxed against the seat. It was a beautiful day and she was with the man she loved. It didn't get much better than this, and she was determined to enjoy the day.

She wasn't looking forward to tonight, though. She had promised Chad that tonight after they visited Dan and had a nice dinner out, they were going back to her house and she was going to tell him about the vision.

She knew what would happen. He wouldn't let her set foot into her shop until Nancy Barelli was caught and behind bars. Chad would probably personally drive her to one of her brothers' homes in Reading.

No, she definitely wasn't looking forward to the confrontation tonight with Chad.

Last night's vision had scared her worse than be-

fore, but for some strange reason she felt Chad had
been safe. It had been a strange yet comforting feeling. As long as Chad was safe, she could handle just
about anything. If she thought the blood on the
shop's floor had been Chad's, she wouldn't let him
cross the threshold. Chad thought Mary had been
out sick on Friday and Saturday, but she had given
Mary the days off with pay. She couldn't take the
chance the blood might be Mary's. Sometime today,
she had to call Mary and tell her not to come in
next week, either.

All that blood had to belong to someone, and she
was trying to eliminate the choices. As of now she had
it down to herself or Nancy Barelli. Once she told
Chad about the vision, The Garden of Eden was either
going to be closed or swarming with undercover police posing as customers.

She raised Chad's hand to her mouth and placed
a kiss on the roughened palm. His hands were large
and strong and had the capability to be violent, but
she wasn't afraid of them. Chad's hands had been
tender and caring as they gave her nothing but pleasure. Her tongue ran the length of one of his fingers
before she gently sucked it into her mouth.

Chad shot her a quick glance before turning into
a parking space in front of her shop. "What are you
doing?"

She playfully bit the tip of his finger before releasing it. "Tasting you."

A shudder shook his body as he turned off the
car and pocketed the keys.

"I love the taste of you." Memories of how they'd

spent the night and most of the morning were still fresh in her mind.

Chad reached for her hand, but she teasingly pulled it out of his reach and opened the door.

"You're playing with fire, Bridget," he growled.

She got out of the car and grinned at him. The fire burning in his eyes made her knees weak as she pulled the keys to the shop from her purse and hurried to the door. "I know."

Chad surveyed the parking lot and the main road. Her protector was always on his guard. This afternoon they were safe. No one could have followed them through the maze of streets he had driven to reach the store. Even if Nancy Barelli was out this very minute looking for them, she wouldn't think to check at the store. It was never open on a Sunday.

Bridget unlocked the door and grinned over her shoulder at Chad. "Maybe I like the way your fire burns."

Chad stepped right in behind her, backed her up against the wall, and kissed her until she could do nothing but cling to him or melt to the floor.

A ragged groan escaped his throat as he broke the kiss and took a step back away from her. "Fires can be dangerous."

"Didn't I tell you? Danger is my middle name."

A fleeting smile teased the corner of his mouth. "I thought it was Erin."

"How am I to have any secrets?" She pouted, but she knew her eyes were smiling. "You know too much about me." She didn't want to keep secrets from Chad, but a little mystery between lovers might not be a bad thing.

Chad leaned forward and kissed away her pout. "I don't know nearly enough, Bridget Erin Mackenzie." His hands were gentle as they pushed her in the direction of the refrigerator units holding her supply of flowers. "But I'm learning. Now get busy and show me what a manly bouquet of flowers looks like. Visiting hours started forty-five minutes ago."

She wrinkled her nose at him, but started to select vases containing different types of flowers. "Do me a favor. Go in the office and get me the roll of dark blue ribbon."

Chad stepped into the back office. His voice reached her as she was pulling another vase from the refrigerator. "Where is it?"

"It's in the box on the desk with a bunch of other ribbons. We just got it in yester . . ."

She whirled around as the front door flew open and the sound of tinkling bells filled the shop.

The knife pressing against her throat stopped her in midturn, and the vase slipped from her hands as Chad appeared in the doorway with his gun drawn. The sound of breaking glass joined the high-pitched giggle from behind her.

Too late, she remembered they hadn't locked the door behind them. They had been too busy kissing.

With a sense of foreboding, she lowered her gaze to the floor and saw the shattered vase, a puddle of water, and three dozen bent and broken daisies. The only thing missing was the blood.

A cold, skinny arm wrapped around her waist, trapping her arms by her side. Nancy Barelli's other hand pressed the knife against her throat so tight that if Bridget swallowed, she would cut her own throat. She couldn't turn to face Barelli, and the sight of the broken vase was too upsetting, so she looked at Chad.

She almost wished she hadn't. The man positioned in the doorway didn't look like the gentle lover from last night or the man who moments before had teased her with burning kisses and promises of fire.

This Chad appeared to be made out of stone. There was a coldness in his eyes she had never seen before, nor wanted to see again. His gun appeared to be aimed straight at her, but she knew it wasn't. Nancy Barelli wasn't a fool. She was using Bridget as a shield and was standing directly behind her. Chad would have to shoot through her to get Barelli.

"Let her go, Nancy." Chad's voice was deep and steady and held nothing but pure malice. If Bridget had been holding the knife on someone, she would have dropped it at the sound of that voice.

Barelli laughed, and the blade scraped against Bridget's tender skin. Bridget clamped her jaw shut against the sting and forced her features not to betray her fear. Chad had enough to worry about if he was going to get them out of this alive.

"I don't think so, Barnett. I want to see your face when I slice her throat."

"You'll be dead before you finish." Chad's cold gaze was locked on the woman behind her right shoulder.

"So will she." The blade pressed harder and

Bridget felt a slight burning sensation, but not excruciating pain.

"I thought you'd want to kill me, Nancy. I'm the one who killed Frank."

"Killing you would be too easy. I wanted to make you suffer first. Like I suffer every day without Frank."

"So you killed my partner."

"I planned to kill your wife and kids first, but you weren't married and you didn't seem to have a girlfriend." The knife pressed harder and Barelli gave a high-pitched laugh. "At the time." Bridget arched her neck back as far as she could to get away from the pressure. "Monterey was choice number two, and he was such an easy target."

"How did you get him out of the car and into the alley?" Chad shot Bridget's throat a fleeting glance, but his gun never wavered.

"Child's play. I jammed a pillow under my coat and pretended to be pregnant. Grabbed my stomach, cried out once or twice before stumbling into the alley. Goody two-shoes was out of the car and meeting his Maker before my second contraction."

Barelli's arm tightened around Bridget. For such a skinny woman, she was amazingly strong. If Bridget tried to break out of her hold, she wouldn't do it without gaining another air hole in her body.

"Heard both your friends lived." Barelli's laugh was slightly wild. "It's a shame. They weren't meant to. I hit them hard. You should have seen them bounce."

Chad's eyes narrowed slightly. "And the fire?"

"Nice touch, wasn't it?" The edge of the knife toyed with the scar already encircling Bridget's throat. "You lost everything you owned. I was going to take your car next, but guess what? You surprised me by moving in with Red here."

Bridget could feel nearly every inch of the woman behind her. Her back was pressed against Barelli's front. She had no room for another retreat if the knife pressed closer. Barelli had about two inches on her own five-foot-six height, but it wasn't enough to give Chad a clear shot.

Chad was waiting for Barelli to make a wrong move. Bridget's gut was telling her that might not happen. Someone's blood was going to flow into the daisies being trampled beneath their feet, and she would rather it not be hers.

Chad couldn't make a move. Barelli was in control of the situation and wasn't likely to screw it up now. That left only her, and her options weren't many. In fact they were damned few. She could think of only one thing to do.

"It took me a while to realize Red here was one of Frank's lady loves." The knife pressed harder, and this time Bridget couldn't control the grimace as pain stung her and a drop of blood rolled down her throat. "How's it feel to know you could never measure up to Frank in her bed?"

Bridget bit her tongue and suppressed the shudder of revulsion threatening to overcome her. Her gaze stayed on Chad, and she witnessed his reaction to either that statement or to the drop of blood flowing down her throat. His finger on the trigger tightened ever so slightly. Chad was going to make his move, and it was up to her to help him.

"I think it's poetic justice that you led me to one of the bitches who stole my Frank away from me."

Bridget contorted her face and drew Chad's glance. She silently mouthed *one*.

"Release her, Nancy. She didn't do anything to you. It's me you want."

Chad glanced at Bridget again, and she mouthed *two*.

"She has to die, Barnett. She stole Frank's love away from me." Barelli seemed to reach some sort of decision. "You only killed his body. She killed his love for me."

Chad glanced at her and she mouthed *three*.

With all her might, she threw herself backward and to the left, away from woman and the blade. Pain streaked across her throat as the gun blasted.

Her arms flailed wildly, but nothing could stop her backward momentum. She connected with the tile floor and pain exploded in her head. Somewhere in the distance, Chad shouted her name.

As her body settled on the hard floor, she slowly turned her head and glanced beside her. A trickle of crimson blood was growing into a river and slowly flowing toward the puddle of water and the trampled daisies.

Chad had reached her side and was still calling her name as he pressed something to her throat. She watched in fascination as the vision unfolded before her. The water turned light pink, then darker pink, then red. Blood red. White daises turned scarlet as a black mist of pain started to obscure the sight.

She reached a hand toward the fading vision and gave Chad what she had promised she would give him today. "There. There it is."

Blackness descended and she never felt her hand drop to the floor.

TWELVE

Chad closed his eyes and forced the sounds of controlled pandemonium from his mind. The thin curtain separating Bridget's cubicle from the rest of the emergency room offered no protection from the noise and cries of other patients.

Bridget was alive. If he could believe the baby-faced doctor who had examined her, she was going to be all right. The doctor hadn't looked old enough to be in college, let alone be graduated from med school.

If Bridget didn't wake up in the next ten minutes, he was getting a second opinion. Hell, maybe he should get a second opinion now.

His captain and what appeared to be half the precinct were out in the waiting room. The media had picked up the story and swarmed around like vultures ready to pick at the dead.

Nancy Barelli had been dead before she hit the floor in Bridget's shop. He couldn't afford to have missed. Bridget's life had depended on that shot.

He still couldn't believe what Bridget had done. If she had been any other person, man or woman, he'd shake her hand and congratulate her on her quick thinking and nerves of steel, but he wanted to wring Bridget's lovely neck for taking such a chance.

If her throat had been in any condition, he might have. As it was, six tiny, delicate stitches had to be sewn across the side of her throat to close the cut the knife had made during her heroic, if not entirely stupid, stunt of throwing herself backward. One of the city's top plastic surgeons had been in the hospital at the time and had done the honors.

Bridget groaned softly and he opened his eyes and watched as she raised a hand to her head. The diagnosis was that she had a concussion and was definitely spending the next twenty-four hours in the hospital. The consensus had been she'd wake up with one heck of a headache. A frown pulled at her mouth, but she didn't open her gorgeous Irish eyes.

Eyes that could see the future.

He'd go to his grave remembering the way she had pointed to the pool of blood and crushed daisies and said, "There it is."

He had known then and there what her vision had been for the past few nights. Bridget hadn't known whose blood would fulfill the vision, yet she had trusted him enough to go into her shop with him. She had known a river of blood would flow, and it had. It could have been hers!

He studied her beautiful face as she softly moaned and tried to open her eyes. It took her a moment, but she did eventually manage the feat. She glanced around the room, bewildered, and then saw him.

He gave her a small, reassuring smile. "You're a hardheaded woman."

"Stubborn." Bridget grimaced and then raised her hand to her throat.

Chad captured her hand and shook his head. "Don't touch." He squeezed her fingers before releasing her hand. "The doctor says you're one lucky woman. The blade missed your larynx by half an inch. We got in a plastic surgeon to do the stitching."

He saw the panic in her eyes and quickly reassured her. "It sounds worse than it was. They were more concerned with scarring than with any medical complications. The doctor assured me the scarring will be minimal."

"The Barellis seem to have had a thing for my throat."

"You have that effect on people." He leaned across the bed and brushed her hair away from her face. "I personally would love to get my hands on it, but I'm controlling that urge." He scowled as he straightened the white sheet covering her. "Barely."

"Barelli's dead, isn't she?"

He slowly nodded. He wasn't going to give her the details and her shop would be good as new before she ever set foot back into it. "You knew, didn't you?"

"Knew what?"

"That Barelli would show up in your shop." He paced to the other side of the room and almost kicked the red hazardous waste container sitting there in frustration.

"I knew you were safe." Her pale hand reached out for him, but he didn't take it. Slowly, it fell back to the cot. "I knew the blood in the vision wasn't yours, Chad. Just like I knew Barelli was connected to that vision."

He thrust his hand through his hair and scowled. "And did you know the blood wasn't yours?"

"No." Freckles stood out against her pale face and pain and confusion clouded her eyes. "You were always with me, Chad. I knew you would be there if something happened. You would keep me safe."

His shout vibrated through the emergency room. "Safe!"

He made a conscious effort to lower his voice when Bridget flinched.

"Is this how I keep you safe? You're in the hospital, there's a half-dozen stitches across your throat, and I just had to shoot a madwoman not six inches away from your stubborn head! Whatever possessed you to think you could trust me? If you trusted me any more, you'd be dead!"

Bridget's eyes shone with tears. "I trust you with my life, Chad."

"Why?"

"Because I love you." A lone tear slipped from the corner of her eye and rolled into her hair.

His heart slammed against his chest. *Bridget loves me!*

Impossible. She was confused and the pain medication was kicking in, that's all. The Bridgets of the world didn't fall in love with disillusioned cops who nearly got them killed whenever they got together. The physical attraction between them was powerful, but that wasn't love. It was strong enough to make him forget to lock the door this afternoon at her shop, a mistake that had nearly cost her her life.

He took a deep breath and slowly shook his head. "No, you don't, Bridget. What you're feeling is gratitude."

"Don't tell me what I'm feeling, Chad. I know the difference between gratitude and love."

"You're seeing me as the man who killed two people who would have killed you, Bridget. I'm not your hero. I'm not anyone's hero."

He had to look away from her eyes and the pain his words were causing. "It's over and done, Bridget. It would be best if we don't see each other again. You need to heal and then get on with your life."

"My Grandmom Rosalie was right about a lot of things, Chad. The future can't be changed, no matter how hard we try. The visions will always come true, but it isn't always bad. Maybe if it hadn't been you in the shop with me this afternoon that would have been my blood. Maybe not." She brushed at the tears overflowing her eyes.

"Five years ago, Grandmom said my visions centered around you. She thought my visions would bring us together and you would end up being the love of my life. I was half in love with you back then. When you didn't visit or call after I was admitted to the hospital, I told her she was wrong. She shrugged, smiled, and said life had a funny way of working things out.

"When the visions started again the other week, I had no choice but to go to you. I knew you would believe me. I wasn't expecting to fall totally in love with you, but I did. I wasn't having those visions because of me, Chad. It was because of you. My visions will always center around those I love, just like my grandmother's have. It's in the blood. It's in the heart."

He turned and gripped the flimsy blue curtain. His knuckles were stark white against the fabric. "You and your grandmother are mistaken, Bridget." He glanced at her quickly over his shoulder and nearly lost his nerve. He almost went to her and begged to be let into her world of color and overprotective families.

He was walking away for her own good. She deserved so much more than he could give her. So far he had managed to get her raped and beaten, choked nearly to death with an electrical cord, and her throat nearly slit—and they hadn't even been on an official date yet.

"I already called your brother Dillon. I'm afraid by the time they settle you in your room upstairs, you'll be overrun by four worried brothers, their wives, and, by the sound of it when I just called, all ten nieces and nephews."

Bridget softly cursed and he had to smile. She was going to hate all that mothering, but he'd rest easier knowing she was in good hands.

He gave her one last look and said, "Take care of yourself, Bridget."

He pulled back the curtain and forced himself to step out of the cubicle and her life.

* * *

Bridget felt another curious stare and knew she couldn't stand there any longer. Half an hour was long enough to lean against the back of Chad's car in the precinct's parking lot. Departing and arriving policemen and women were starting to give her some pretty strange looks.

She didn't blame them. Chad should have been here forty minutes ago. What was keeping him? He was going to blow her perfect timetable.

In the seven days since she'd been released from the hospital, she'd thought of nothing but Chad. He had been right about her family's invading her hospital room and her home.

When she'd been released, they had deposited her on the couch in her living room and announced they had a plan. She had panicked. She always panicked when all four of her brothers put their heads together and agreed on one course of action. It usually spelled disaster for her.

Their parents were out of the country. No one notified them of her latest scrape with danger, since she was well on the road to recovery. Her brothers had wanted the whole problem settled before their parents came home. They were all chipping in and giving her money to start a new Garden of Eden up in Reading.

She had politely declined their generous offer. Then she had more strenuously refused. Finally, she had to point-blank threaten never to babysit another niece or nephew again if they didn't all pack up and go home. She wasn't selling her home or her business.

She told them she was tired and wanted to rest. What she wanted to do was think. Her brothers, after stocking her refrigerator, measuring the dining room for its planned renovation, and giving her car an oil change, finally packed up and went home.

Chad loved her. She knew it with the same clarity she knew she loved him. A combination of pride and guilt had made him walk away from her in the emergency room. He still felt guilty for failing her, which was just plain ridiculous. She didn't know how to force him to see he had never failed her. She had seen the pain and guilt flash in his eyes when his gaze had landed on the thick bandage that had been around her throat.

Well, the bandage was gone now and the doctor had taken the stitches out in his office that afternoon. The cut had been three inches long and a half an inch above the scar already encircling her throat. With a little more time to heal properly, it would be barely noticeable. Chad would just have to get used to seeing both scars.

But Chad was still carrying the scars of his childhood. She had picked that up by the way he avoided talking about his past or his upbringing. She'd noticed the near awe and the longing in his voice every time he mentioned her large family.

He wanted a family of his own. With his background, he just didn't know how to go about getting one. His profession didn't help the situation. Everyone knew the divorce rate among cops was staggeringly high. Add the dangers he encountered almost daily, and she could almost sympathize with his reasoning. Almost.

She had tried on several occasions to tell Chad he hadn't failed her. In truth, she had failed him by dragging him into her own personal hell every time she had a vision. Chad wasn't listening. So instead of fighting the past, she was going to fight for the future.

Bridget glanced at the precinct building across the street, took a deep breath, and decided to confront the lion in his den. She'd hoped the first part of her plan would take place in the semiprivacy of the parking lot, but if not . . . she wasn't known for being stubborn for nothing.

Five minutes later, she stood in the center of the busy room and stared at the man she loved. Chad hadn't seen her yet, but every cop in the room knew who she was and who she was there to see.

Chad looked as bad as she felt. He sat behind a desk tapping a pencil, staring out the window, and apparently pondering the fate of the world. Lord, how she missed him.

She walked up to his desk and silently stood there waiting. She didn't have to wait long. Chad sensed her presence and turned. "Bridget! What are you doing here?"

"I need to report a crime." She sat on the edge of the seat of an old wooden chair next to his desk. She wasn't sure if he was happy to see her, but he definitely was surprised.

She lowered her voice to a near whisper. They were already attracting too much attention. "I'm a precognitive clairvoyant and someone has stolen my heart. I can see the future, but without my heart, what good is it?"

The pencil in Chad's hand dropped to the floor. "Have you seen the future?"

This was the part she worried about. She had to lie to Chad, and she was a terrible liar. "I've been having a vision lately." She glanced out the window that had held his attention so thoroughly moments before. "It's a room, a baby's room. It's painted in yellow and white stripes and there must be three dozen clowns all over the place. There's a white crib near the window. A mobile with more clowns is slowly turning around playing some musical tune. It's capturing the baby's attention."

"Baby?" Chad's voice was a small croak.

"Yes. There's a baby in the crib, but I can't tell if it's a boy or a girl. I feel the love, though. The baby is surrounded by love."

She glanced at Chad and clutched her purse tighter. He seemed to be in shock.

She quickly stood up to make her escape. The privacy of the parking lot would have been better, much better. She hurried from the room and felt every gaze upon her as Chad bellowed her name. She didn't turn or slow down until she reached her car and had to unlock it.

With trembling hands and a racing heart, she drove home to put the second part of her plan into motion.

One thought plagued her for the entire fifteen-minute drive: *What if he doesn't come?*

* * *

Chad pulled in behind Bridget's car, cut the engine, and headed for her house. He didn't bother knocking, but opened the door and called her name. "Bridget?"

He headed for the kitchen and came to a sudden stop when he noticed the table was set for two, complete with a lace tablecloth and burning candles.

Bridget was pulling something out of the microwave with one hand and inserting something else with the other. "I'm surprised you didn't get a ticket. You must have run every red light between the precinct and here."

He blinked at the domestic scene. Even Shamrock was curled up fast asleep by the patio doors.

"You're pregnant!" The whole time he had been driving it was the only thought to penetrate his bewildered mind. Bridget was pregnant. She was carrying his child! He was going to become a daddy. They would be married by the end of the week, or, if she insisted on a big wedding, the end of the month.

Bridget shook her head and placed a bowl of steaming mashed potatoes on the table. "No." A seductive smile curved her generous mouth. "At least not yet."

"What do you mean, no?" Disappointment pressed against his heart. Bridget wasn't carrying his child. He wasn't going to be a daddy. When the hell had he decided he wanted to become a daddy?

"I lied to you about the vision. I told you before

the visions don't happen with the good stuff of life. No births, no weddings, and no lottery numbers. The good things in life will just have to surprise us, I guess."

"You're not having any more visions?" What was she up to?

Lord, he couldn't believe how much he had missed her. Not thirty minutes ago he had been staring out a window wondering how she was doing, running through his list of reasons why he had walked away from her in the emergency room. Most of them weren't making any sense.

"No visions." The beep from the microwave caught her attention. She picked up pot holders and carefully pulled a dish from the oven and set it on the table. "Are you staying for dinner? It's meatloaf and mashed potatoes."

He remembered the conversation he'd had with her a while back about not finding Mrs. Right because cops make extremely bad husbands and that he would have nothing to talk about to a wife over the meatloaf and mashed potatoes. Bridget had made some comment about what a pair of misfits they were, the cop and the clairvoyant. She had also referred to her imaginary husband as her meatloaf partner.

Was all this a coincidence? He stared at the table and knew it wasn't. Bridget was trying to tell him something. "I've never known you to be shy, Bridget." He waved his hand at the table. "Out with it."

"I'm giving you a vision, Chad."

"A vision of what?"

"Your future." Bridget's gaze held nothing but

love. "If you want it, that is." Her hands were clasped together. "Meatloaf on Wednesday nights. A baby in a clown-filled nursery." A frown pulled at her mouth. "Better make it babies. We Mackenzies tend to have large families."

Babies! Bridget was talking about having his babies. He should be running so fast and so far he'd be in Arizona before catching his breath. So why did it sound like heaven to him?

He never knew how much he'd wanted to be a dad until Bridget described that vision to him. Hell, he could practically see the kids' green eyes. More important, he realized he couldn't let Bridget out of his life. He loved her, and he would have eventually tracked her down to tell her so if she hadn't appeared at the precinct today. "You'd marry a cop?"

"No, I'd marry a man who just happens to be a cop." She played nervously with the hem of her sweater. "You'd marry a clairvoyant?"

"No, I'd marry a woman who just happens to be a clairvoyant." He had lost his heart the first time he had ever kissed her. He should have accepted it sooner. He took two steps closer and blew out the candles.

"What are you doing?"

"Blowing out the candles." He frowned at the delicious meal Bridget had prepared. It was a real shame it was going to go to waste.

"Why?"

"They're a fire hazard." He took a step toward her and swung her up into his arms. She felt like heaven.

He glanced around the kitchen to make sure nothing was left on.

"What are you doing?" Bridget wrapped her arms around his neck as he walked out of the kitchen and headed for the stairs. She didn't sound too concerned.

"We're starting on that baby." His mouth brushed hers as he entered her bedroom. "I've never made a baby before, so I might need some practice." He grinned down at her upturned face. "Lots of practice."

Bridget bounced in the center of her bed when he released her. Her flowing skirt billowed in the air and then settled around her calves. A wide grin lit her face. "What about the meatloaf?"

"Screw the meatloaf, Bridget. It's you I want." His serious gaze locked with hers. "I've been fighting it for a long time now."

"Fighting what?"

He lowered himself on top of her and nipped at her tempting mouth. "Loving you." His mouth slanted across hers for a kiss that should have set off her smoke detectors. He pulled back and stared into her desire-filled eyes. He could actually see his future in their depths. "I love you, Bridget Erin Mackenzie. Make me the happiest man alive and become my wife, my love, and the mother of my children."

Her determined fingers reached up and pulled his head back down to her waiting mouth. "I thought you'd never ask."

BOOK YOUR PLACE ON OUR WEBSITE AND MAKE THE READING CONNECTION!

We've created a customized website just for our very special readers, where you can get the inside scoop on everything that's going on with Zebra, Pinnacle and Kensington books.

When you come online, you'll have the exciting opportunity to:

- View covers of upcoming books
- Read sample chapters
- Learn about our future publishing schedule (listed by publication month *and author*)
- Find out when your favorite authors will be visiting a city near you
- Search for and order backlist books from our online catalog
- Check out author bios and background information
- Send e-mail to your favorite authors
- Meet the Kensington staff online
- Join us in weekly chats with authors, readers and other guests
- Get writing guidelines
- AND MUCH MORE!

**Visit our website at
http://www.zebrabooks.com**

COMING IN NOVEMBER
FROM BOUQUET ROMANCES

#21 Sweet Sensations by Adrienne Basso

__(0-8217-6409-8, **$3.99**) Writing the definitive dessert cookbook is more than enough to keep Lauren Stuart busy until she must investigate the wealthy hunk who has claimed her cheesecake as his own in a magazine article. But when she meets Jonathon Windsor, she's surprised to find that he's a delicious temptation of another kind!

#22 Jenny's Star by Patricia Werner

__(0-8217-6410-1, **$3.99**) Still smarting over a failed romance and anticipating a lonely holiday far from her family, Jenny Knight can't help wishing Christmas was over...until sexy, green-eyed Parker McAllister turns up. Now Jenny knows what she *really* wants for Christmas—a chance to win this wonderful man's heart.

#23 Heart Song by Jane Kidder

__(0-8217-6411-X, **$3.99**) When the world famous pianist Alexei Romanov asked his lovely young student Natalie Worthington to accompany him back to the Soviet Union, she could not give up her career goals for such a drastic move. Now, seven years later, Natalie and Alex meet again. Can they continue to deny their passion?

#24 A Christmas Bouquet by Suzanne Barrett, Kate Holmes, and Vella Munn

__(0-8217-6412-8, **$3.99**) Christmas is a time filled with mistletoe—and miracles. In this trio of cozy romances, three Bouquet authors introduce strong-willed heroines who unexpectedly discover the most precious gift of all . . . love.

Call toll free **1-888-345-BOOK** to order by phone or use this coupon to order by mail.

Name _____
Address _____
City _____ State _____ Zip _____
Please send me the books I have checked above.
I am enclosing $_____
Plus postage and handling* $_____
Sales tax (where applicable) $_____
Total amount enclosed $_____
*Add $2.50 for the first book and $.50 for each additional book.
Send check or Money order (no cash or CODs) to:
Kensington Publishing Corp., 850 Third Avenue, New York, NY 10022
Prices and Numbers subject to change without notice. Valid only in the U.S.
All books will be available 10/1/99. All orders subject to availability.
Check out our web site at **www.kensingtonbooks.com**

Put a Little Romance in Your Life With
Fern Michaels

__Dear Emily   0-8217-5676-1 $6.99US/$8.50CAN

__Sara's Song   0-8217-5856-X $6.99US/$8.50CAN

__Wish List   0-8217-5228-6 $6.99US/$7.99CAN

__Vegas Rich   0-8217-5594-3 $6.99US/$8.50CAN

__Vegas Heat   0-8217-5758-X $6.99US/$8.50CAN

__Vegas Sunrise   1-55817-5983-3 $6.99US/$8.50CAN

__Whitefire   0-8217-5638-9 $6.99US/$8.50CAN